for

Lilian Beatrice Nichols, t.a.d.

Roses are flowering in Picardy
But there's never a rose like you

F. E. Weatherley

Acknowledgements

Jane Hess (Toronto) for steering me to *Dimbola;* Dr. Brian Hinton, MBE, Hon. Curator, Julia Margaret Cameron Trust (U.K.), for sharing J.M.C. & Tennyson lore; the staff of *Dimbola Lodge, Farringford,* and the *Albion Hotel,* all at Freshwater Bay, I.O.W., for making research a delight; the Watts Gallery, Compton, Surrey (U.K.), for inspiration; Marita Clarke, London (U.K.) for her character and numerous local pointers; Dr. Ron Gerridzen (Ottawa) for ensuring this wasn't a posthumous publication; Frank Rodgers (Ottawa) for numerous suggestions and support; Prof. Jack Granatstein, OC (Toronto) for reading and comments; the spirits of the Freshwater Circle; and lastly, dear Liz, for so much.

Part I

Over There

(1)

And the faces of the Sisters and the glory in their eyes

Rudyard Kipling

October 25, 1899
<u>Quebec City</u>

A brilliant 'Indian summer' afternoon had drawn a crowd onto the Dufferin Terrace for a stroll. Amongst the throng of raw recruits, proud families, local merchants, longshoremen, and careening children, a wiry young clerk from Lévis cruised back and forth, gawking at the females.

It was a still creature, however, clasping the black railing at the edge, as if at sea, that stopped René Hébert dead in his tracks. Long hair was pulled up in glistening, pre-Raphaelite piles, and the weak sun tinged fine cheekbones. She seemed oblivious to the promenade behind as her cobalt eyes fixed on a large steamer loading at the government docks in Lower Town. Starched white collar and cuffs accented the Prussian cape and long navy-wool skirt which marked her as a nursing sister; the eyes and apple complexion branded her an *anglaise*.

René was 17, but she couldn't have been much older so he sidled over to her left, where he kicked the base of the railing a few times.

" Ma'amzelle, please, tell me your name. "

Her full mouth, with its bemused smile as she turned towards him, held René an instant captive. He had no idea why, but this woman waved the key to his immediate future, and he suddenly longed to be under that cape, with his head on what looked to be ample breasts, listening raptly to her advice. For all that was settled in his life was that shaping hulls in his late father's *chalouperie*, eating *patates* and belching songs in dock taverns, was not to be the way and the light for René Hébert.

" If I said, 'Florence Nightingale', would it mean anything ? "

It didn't, though 'Florence' had clear euphony even in French. " Non, Ma'amzelle ", answered René, undeterred.

" Well, it's not my name – it's my *inspiration.* " As she spoke, her hands gripped the balustrade more firmly, their gracefulness unshackled by gloves. " In a few days, I sail for Cape Town with the volunteers. See, that's the boat down there, the *Sardinian.* I have to do my part: there'll be wounds to tend to, and they say the climate positively *grows* disease. "

The normally cocky René was at a loss for words. He'd heard of the rough contingent now massing at Quebec, but all he knew was the Queen had yanked her Imperial chain and the anglos were off to some folly overseas. And, most Quebeckers gave a damn.

The fledgling lamp-lady softened at René's awkwardness.

" Why haven't *you* joined up ? You look fit. I'm sure we'd have *lots* to talk about if you were in uniform. " She started to move off.

" Mais, ma'amzelle… "

" Of course, my name. Remember it now: 'Minnie', " and she patted his elbow encouragingly.

Jingoistic rallies and posters had worked magic elsewhere in the country, but the time and paper wasn't wasted in French Canada. Yet here, within seconds, this dedicated siren had launched René's ship of war.

René stared at the flame-red leaves blowing across the boardwalk, and saw them meld into a soldier's tunic.

**

There is a lady sweet and kind
Was never a face so pleased my mind;
I did but see her passing by,
And yet I love her till I die

Anon.

He saw her once more, on the evening of the 30th, when, to tremendous fanfare, they sailed out of Lower Town for South Africa. At about 8:00 p.m., Minnie glided round the corner of the *Sardinian*'s aft upper deck on the arm of an officer: Major Pelletier, the very same who'd taken pity that morning on the underage but eager René, and contrary to all regulations, and mostly to win favour with his beautiful companion, hustled him aboard with last-minute supplies – and that was it.

He never learned whether Minerva Affleck survived the anvil heat, or if, as many Sisters, she fell to typhoid, dysentery, or shrapnel somewhere in the veldt. He was crushed, but would never have let her know, and swore to honour his commitment.

God grant him, there would be others, a prayer which carried René through the late afternoon of 'Black Sunday', February 18, 1900, at a grim niche called Paardeberg Drift, where the 1st Royal Canadians hurled themselves across the Modder River in gallant futility. At 5:30 p.m., an expanding Mauser bullet ripped through his right lung and he wavered in a stifling tent for three weeks before being invalided to England.

The water which sustained him in that first critical period came from the Modder, choked with bloated men, horses, and Boer excrement. Enteric fever struck just as the ambulance packet docked in Southampton, and the young 'Frenchie' was promptly whisked over the Solent to convalesce on the Isle of Wight.

René seemed back from the ashes, however, when he impregnated Charlotte Nichols, a British Sister charmed by his accent and boyish *élan*. He still coughed easily, at the lightest breeze, but in June, they embarked together for Halifax and Quebec City, and Charlotte gave birth to twins on December 20th.

Her family in Haslemere railed bitterly, until three years later.

**

It was November, 1902, just prior to Jo and Lil's second birthday, when Char first noticed the stains. Three weekends in a row, she discovered pink flecks down the front of his Sunday shirts.

Sundays had become René's escape. Char saw it in his eyes: he looked older than a 20 year-old should look, but she hadn't the heart to bar the door. After Mass, he'd rush down the hill for the ferry from Lévis to Lower Town; then, sweating, he'd trudge up the winding street to Dufferin Terrace, and when he'd stopped wheezing, would pace for hours, pausing to watch the ships come and go, waiting impatiently for the next war and Minnie's lovely urging.

But neither came and René grew more distracted. He doted on the twins, but drifted up from the warehouse in the evening as if he no longer really belonged, and they were just tiny players in some vaguely familiar tableau.

After Christmas, René started training for Carnaval with the Montmorency boat team. Three days a week in January and early February, he rowed and scrambled through the ice-choked St. Lawrence, torturing Char with his fevered skin and horrendous night cough. He said it killed a lot of the ragging from childhood friends for having 'sold out' to the English. In any event, there was no denying him; she understood that. She was already an awkward prize.

It was -35° F and blizzard conditions on race day. The beacon at Lévis, first of three touch points on the course, was just a yellow blob in a white nightmare. The St. Michel and Montmorency boats collided on the last leg directly below the government docks, sending René into the water. He managed to claw back in and they finished a sensational second, but he lapsed almost immediately into delirium and a coal wagon was commandeered to get him up to the Hôtel Dieu. Seven days later, he died of pneumonia.

**

René had been the only son and heir. The clan at Lévis wasted no time in purging his foreign interlude. In less than a week, the Hébert family determined that Charlotte should returnto England, without the boy. The little girl, fetching as she was with her Wedgwood complexion, only mirrored the ill-wind stranger who'd blown into their midst.

No one suggested the *anglaise* find work at the hospital. Even as she mourned in one wing of the *maison Hébert*, Char lost her wish to have René buried on a sheltered slope with other vets; instead, they pressed him into a wind-scraped hill, to be forever scolded by weeping Virgins and bleeding Christs.

It was cruel, perverse even, but disillusioned and bereft – not to mention dependent on the Héberts for passage home – Char agreed to say nothing to her daughter about a twin sibling until her eighteenth birthday. Once on board, March 1st, Char tried valiantly to rationalize not seeing Jo, and of course, in his dark, dancing eyes, René. There was always the hope things might resolve themselves with distance, and the children be reunited sooner…

Char pressed her child's face into her shawl, as if to hide the shore and erase any memory of this time. Her Lil would *never* wander overseas.

Manoir de Mauvide-Genest
Île d'Orléans

(2)

Manoir Mauvide-Genest,
Île d'Orléans, Quebec City
October 15, 2000

Cannon thundered below. Its black shot tore up through the scarlet maples edging the great river of New France, and the shock seemed to lift Marie Rioux bodily from her wrought-iron chair. For the first time in her thirty-five years, Marie started with the rage that had haunted the air since 1759, when the residents tore out like angry bees to pop their muskets at James Wolfe and his British fleet, fighting the ebb of the St. Lawrence.

Two and a half centuries later, the scars lingered in the Quebec psyche: imagined, exploited, occasionally physical. Marie had only to look over her cup of tazo tea at the south wall of the Manoir, at the unpatched pock-marks where the young Major General had replied with 16-pounders.

As it happened, this tea with its unscheduled bang, the product of an agitated reverie, marked the opening *and* closing salvo in a real struggle. When the 'smoke' cleared later that afternoon, something truer stood and beckoned Marie.

**

A failed flower-child, in awe of her daughter's will, her mother managed only a conventional reply.

" Honey, you can't just drop out like this...*totally.* "

But the new path, irresistible, lay in a clean break from almost everything and everyone. It led, for starters, out the door of a budding career in provincial politics and the never-buried angst of Quebec nationalism. The pitchmen urging her generation to the barricades against the '*maudits anglais*' impressed her now as miners in a black hole. If she had to be 'oppressed', as they urged, it was damn well not going to be via someone else's adopted martyrdom. Let the Mauvide family rattle ancient sabres, but she no longer felt any urge to remind the world that Marie Rioux, twice-crowned '*La Reine du Carnaval'*, refused to hate English-Canada *eternally* for a French defeat by the British over two hundred and forty years ago.

At the same time, Marie felt guilty that her advocate's zeal for the little guy had waned considerably, drained by the banality of crime and punishment. It wasn't as petty as the narc detectives coming onto her all the time, it was more the ingrained attitude that defence counsel were somehow no better than their clientele, and, the annoying inclination to agree, especially after wretched coffee interviews with pedophiles or rapists. She knew better, of course, intellectually, but there was no one stoking her home-fires, anxious to absorb her frustration or spark new dreams.

She needed a fresh start, a vibrant, mysterious cause.

Ironically, it was an anglophone writer, Callaghan, who said something years before at one of her McGill lectures that filtered back – perhaps because of her musical bent – something about life being a violin with more than one string, and it should be played accordingly.

Such was the declaration of independence steeped in Marie's autumn tea. She didn't flog it as a talk-show revelation or filler for a weekend travel section; it was simply her own next step, conveyed by mind and circumstance. From that afternoon, Marie found herself re-orchestrating. She began looking past the usual, beyond merely down-river, across oceans.

Her one misgiving arose from allegiance to her 'special place', floating east of the city, an irrational fear it might crumble because she abandoned it.

Built in 1734 for a royal surgeon near the south bank of Île d'Orléans, and in latter years a *musée* with a patio for teas, the Manoir and the island had served faithfully as Marie's other-world. In childhood, it poked through the snow-fog in a Maurice Cullen painting above her bed. In her teens, it was sanctuary from Catholic dogma on sticky summer days and September afternoons. Out she would pedal from Basse Ville on her Lady Schwinn, several kilometers to the Pont de l'Île, beckoned by tree-draped roads, circling water that flowed to the Atlantic, and of course, the Manoir, and Madame Bédard's hot raisin scones.

It was the only touchstone Marie felt guilty deserting, so it would travel with her, visualized on her ring finger. As for her mother, she adored her, but her mother was content with local waters, whereas Marie had pledged to swimming on.

Two days later, Marie blew in and out of her law office in under forty-five minutes: all it took to calm Jean-Pierre Nöel, her partner, assure him he had her unqualified trust, instruct him to shuffle her files with his, rough up a notional share and credit a new account with the 'proceeds'. He could send a nice draft accordingly via 'General Delivery', London. She unframed her degrees and rolled them up, on the very remote chance she might someday flaunt her wares in another jurisdiction.

She avoided insulting J-P by not confessing what she really felt, that for her, litigation and its gamesmanship had grown tawdry. She fibbed instead, wailing that she was bravely sacrificing herself, 'going ahead to explore mid-life crisis', and vowed to report back.

The rest was easier: resigning from various women's coalitions; rejecting a flood of pleas to stay and run for public office. *The new millennium is here, Marie.* And so it was, untrussed by any 1759 battle on the Plains of Abraham. The process freaks and vernacular of 'empowerment' made her gag: honey, just *carpe* the *diem* and get on with a life ! At lunch towards the end, she surprised herself and rankled cronies by ordering a second *crème fraiche* and espresso and whispering confidentially, 'Of course, the quest for 44 double-D and buns of titanium can be pursued *any*where.'

Her decision caused a brief whirlwind, but friends and colleagues faded all too quickly into a distant room. Few doubted Marie's sincerity, though some challenged her slash and burn approach. But it wasn't being fickle, only unfulfilled, and the clean slate was truly seductive once engaged. It was exhilarating in fact, the cold cutting of legal and sundry ties, the choosing and planning to make do for a year, *or for the rest of my life*. Less and less remained to hold her back. She took long, pensive runs down the Grande Allée and Rue St. Louis into the old town, dubbing them, 'Marie, the Farewell Tour'. Along the way, she imagined her trainers pounding out the ashes of her marriage; then later, showered and flushed, glistening with fresh perspective, she hit *Le Gaulois* to complete the purging with pints of *La Fin du Monde*. The Final Run ended with her kissing nearly every street artist on the Rue du Trésor – abdicating as their champion in countless *pro bono* battles with local bureaucrats.

In all the flurry, she hadn't stopped to consider the actual moment of departure. When it came, Marie had to weather an emotional 'sail-past'. Childhood shores eventually receded, as did her tears, but not before throwing out a link with others who'd also left. She didn't sail alone.

**

October 31, 2000
Cour Supérieure, Quebec City

" No.7 on the list Your Honour: 'Richard Garnet'. "

" Where's your lawyer Mr. Garnet ? "

Garnet had no idea, and he was anxious to get his trial over with; it was Rioux, after all, who'd urged a fight from the start, two fire-bombed windows notwithstanding. '*A court challenge is critical, Mr. Garnet. Every book-seller has a right to advertise in English. Screw the Crown; the pen is mightier than the blunt instrument.'*

Garnet suddenly felt sheepish for not paying up his retainer; he'd left a recent letter unopened on the assumption it was a fee reminder, and he'd quit answering phone calls because of threats.

Otherwise, he'd have known that his counsel sailed that same day, and that one, J-P Nöel, had been dealt his cause.

**

Marie hugged the port rail of the *FRANZ JOSEF* to ground a sudden light-headedness. The Citadel, daubed with the sand-castle turrets of the Chateau Frontenac, slipped away to the stern. To its right stood the Ursuline convent, skirts pulled tightly about General Montcalm's skull, and then Basse Ville, cluttered below the cliffs, and finally, farther east, Bassin Louise, with tugs darting in and out. Away slipped Marie's old world.

Her gaze tracked south across the St. Lawrence, beneath the 10,000 frozen voices cheering racers over February floes to Lévis. The shouts gave way to the wooden wheels and horse hooves of *calèches* on cobblestone at the top of Rue St. Jean – *God*, the passionate tours she'd had there on summer evenings ! And the teenage boys from New England, bouncing among the pretty street *artistes*, intent on foreign conquest, vying with serious young Montréalais in ratty black turtlenecks and sucking foul *Gauloises*, trying desperately to look like Belmondo or Depardieu.

A grey tern, drafting off the ship above a cloak of shrieking gulls, brought her mother to mind, and Marie smiled at the image of the dear woman skating hell-bent over Dufferin Terrace to rescue her after a fall on the *patinoir*. She'd been weepy during last night's dinner at *Aux Anciens*, but perked up with a promise that Marie would 'stop and listen to every nightingale' in England, and not forget the way home.

No touching image of her father sailed out.

He'd absconded in the late '60s to found a sun-cult near Montreux, and never returned. Her mother reverted soon after to her maiden name, 'Rioux'; though it was a bundle of his scammed money, sent back in a moment of remorse and dumped immediately by her mother into a trust, which now swelled Marie's travel fund.

Marie pulled her mom's Norwegian sweater over short chestnut hair and well-toned upper body, distracting several deckhands.

Even more bracing than the air was the unknown. Casting off with no fixed agenda seemed perfect: ancient pubs, rivers, village registers, graveyards, strangers and other yet-undetermined guideposts could map an English itinerary. Every road taken throws up its own intrigue. Her rationale was restless, but sound. It wasn't as if a sudden interest in ceramics had dragged her off to 'winter' at San Miguel De Allende with face-lifted ex-pats and glitterati.

Marie pushed a delete button, and in the crystal evening, defaulted irrevocably from Ms Terrific to… *wandervogel*.

The word, shelved over 15 years, fell dreamily from her tongue: *wandervogel*, wonderful ! It ushered back the clamour and smoke of student bistros in Old Montreal – what was her motto then ? As Île d'Orléans drew closer on the port, Marie chanted into the light wind, " *lean, lawless, aimless...with rucksack, without papers, without official existence...* " The 'lawless' bit appealed even more than in her freshman year and first reading of Evelyn Waugh's *When The Going Was Good.*

College days had gone astray, but tonight...tonight, there was no denying the going was great. And, she was gone.

" Is interesting, this woman, arguing with the air. "

Marie turned to face a younger, stocky male, holding rags and brass-cleaner, planted a respectful distance behind and to her left. His eyes wandered over her, but he seemed harmless. *Hey, you should see me in court.*

" Just saying goodbye to a lot of ghosts... "

" You are student maybe ? "

Why not ? Once again, and of the world... however it comes. And she turned back to the land sliding by. The night she veered onto her new course, Marie drifted off watching Bogart and Astor steam into the Pacific. The deckhand's blunt question confirmed her own passage.

Along the shore, lights burst like random pin-holes through the gathering dark. The *FRANZ JOSEF* pulled even with the mid-point of Île d'Orleans, where the great sloping roof of a cherished building caused her eyes to brim. *Poor Mme Bédard...* she'd wasted horribly in recent years and no longer recognized the school-girl on the bicycle. *Good night dear lady…*and Marie looked away.

“ I am Polska and ”

The sailor hadn’t moved.

“ …like student also. I am reading all of ”

Ma foi, non. Not another…

“ Joseph Conrad. ”

“ Really ? ” *Let’s skip the typhoon bit.* “ He’s very serious isn’t he, so dark. ”

Marie thought she must have been nautical at heart as she felt unconfined, in fact, freed, by the moving deck. She let herself stare at her fellow ‘student’. A gangway lamp burnished the fair hair on his arms and chest. Jean Luc had been concave and generally hairless. She reflected how they’d never truly made love; it was more like he inflicted it...

The Citadel still in sight and her libido already cruising. A tingle ran through her body without disapproval. The last of her trousseau cartwheeled into the foam astern, leaving Marie barely in contact with the deck. She looked up at the stars and reached out drowsily for them.

“ Do me a favour ? ”

The Polish extrovert was all ears.

“ My cabin’s # 24. When we get close to Tadoussac, please knock loudly. I don’t want to miss the whales. ”

(3)

Portsmouth, England
November 12, 2000

Sam Neale lunged into the raw morning air, cursing.

It never failed. Every fucking time he checked in at British Andorra Tobacco, he left demeaned, wilted by treatment as some sort of vile accessory. Once again, minor aspirations had garnered no respect. Outside the head office, he rubbed the linen of his Armani suit and tie, even checking the shine on his tassled loafers. The spiffy duds had lost their cachet and now felt constricting; he was sweating at the collar.

It pissed him off. They were no better, these *Pimms* and Beamer fairies. Maybe they were Number 2 in the world, but if you peeled off the hype, they were scum on the same water, merchants of death to millions of spotty youth, targeted and 'executed' no less than any wayward employee or corporate adversary under one of his contracts.

He'd been loyal for a decade now, as loyal as henchmen come, and still the gits barred him from exotic F1 racing venues on B.A.'s logo-flogging junkets. They even shunned him in the champagne tent at Ascot and Wimbledon. They made it plain:

he had no daylight existence; he was a dark tool – albeit a lethal one – for promoting fidelity. Christ, what happened to honour among thieves ?

A ray of personal guilt shot from the cold sun, which he easily deflected.

Their edge was an ability to polish a black trade into prestige: what was *his* ? His neck began to dry as he remembered the goods he had on British Andorra. Some day he'd cash in, and he gloated at the east-African memo from New Business Group he'd once accidentally seen and copied: '*These people are unsophisticated, inferior, vulnerable – go get' em Marketing !*'

The media would move like a scythe through the peerage with that one.

His summons from Damian Prinsep followed, within minutes, the delivery of the morning paper and the published heresy of two of B.A.'s directors. The press was first out of the gate, so it was too late to cut them off at the pass or have the heretics smeared as ingrates. Worse, they were both too senior to be credibly disavowed as 'rogue' elements, an otherwise useful label applied to numerous tobacco mafiosi and two-bit middlemen from Dubai to Singapore.

" Don't suppose you read the *Times*, Neale, " British Andorra's Director of Internal Affairs had begun, more by way of assertion than query, " ...outrageous affront to the shareholders ! " But that capped the moral huff – and as if Neale gave a rat's ass – the real party line following in fuzzier terms of pounds sterling.

Some wretched journalist had evidently tapped a vein of disaffection in the research wing of the NBG. Prinsep ground his teeth, guessing how the muckraker had preyed on the directors' finer instincts, trolling for a made-in-Britain 'insider'. And bloody devastating it would be if he'd landed one. Not all the beans were out of the bag, yet, but the 'devastation' Prinsep feared jeopardized millions of pounds of hard-bought image.

The industry's Jacob Marley chains were dragging loudly. The good old '*walk a mile for a Camel*' days were just that, history, west of the new republics anyway. Adverse jury verdicts in the U.S., Australia, and Italy of all places, continued to vent the spleen of next-of-kin, though it wasn't the astronomical awards that hurt – they could be relentlessly appealed down – it was the now-routine bad press. Throw in almost daily revelations of tobacco-smuggling cartels and purchased science, a showy new health crusade at the WHO, and B.A., along with the other giants, was being driven east, its western virginity ravaged for all to see.

There were some attempts to mitigate. After sloughing the gargantuan face cost of their 'settlement' in the U.S. onto the consumer, the mega-nationals had bonded to promote an 'anti-youth smoking' campaign in Europe and North America – thus enshrining nicotine as an 'adult choice' and rite of passage – but such intrigue notwithstanding, the rosy tobacco clime continued to mist.

Further scandal was just no longer fiscally tenable. When the *Times* broke the story that morning that B.A. had been working on nitrosamine extraction, carbon filters, palladium, and other carcinogenic blocks, with the goal of producing a 'safer' fag, *decades* before, the sky truly began to fall.

Even then, the media exposé was not of itself fatal. In-house spin doctors could always fabricate an ethical agenda which had compelled B.A. scientists to keep things low-profile until 'perfected', so as not to raise 'false expectations'. But the crusher would come when it emerged that company policy had suppressed early break-throughs in favour of retaining the unmodified product with its 'buzz', and consequently, keeping the addicted in the brand fold. Slapping 'light' and 'mild' on the pack had been a later brainwave that played to nascent health concerns, while actually hooking new smokers, mainly female. Women had manufactured their own 'safe' cigarette.

On such issues of public confidence, B.A. dispensed with protocol, and those few with access to the big picture huddled in its star chamber. In raw terms, this put the Chairman's goon squad on alert, and thus, on occasion, Sam Neale – he of the face '*well-worn with evil passion*' (the view of Molly, Prinsep's secretary, who had twice her boss' education).

If essential, Prinsep had no qualms about activating violence. It was all there anyway, for Christ's sake, embedded in the template of every B.A. contract for personnel above the status of clerk, all there in years of learning to tow a socially dubious line. Personally, he was all for just locking the buggers into a rail commuter and banking on their probable death in a 'leaves-on-the-track' disaster.

Neale, however, was the minion he was officially charged with triggering. Neale was the corporate instrument for delivering delicate ultimatums – ones that mentioned wives and children, future aspirations – which, if unheeded, generated extreme prejudice.

**

A curl of rich sea air enticed Neale down towards the Royal Naval yard, and inevitably, the *Still and West*, a venerable pub which gazed from its own little spit over the Solent to Ryde and the Isle of Wight.

Neale settled in by a large window with the *Telegraph* and enough lager to bridge the early afternoon. Whenever the morning's encounter, and his bile, threatened to re-surface, he would peer sideways from his paper at the slate-green expanse roiling behind the freighters coming in off the Atlantic. Back towards another world he'd once inhabited.

He didn't waste time examining his new mission documents. At first blush, the subjects appeared weak and vulnerable and he anticipated little trouble bringing them round. The 'urgent' dictates of Prinsep could wait, at least until approximately 5:00 p.m., for Neale had one laudatory quirk: he worshipped opera; in particular, spellbinding arias. The noble deeds, the passion and tragedy, the musical elevation of words beyond mere communication, complemented his own sphere.

Puccini's *Turandot* was playing Portsmouth today, and today only. Armageddon itself would not deter Neale's attendance.

The Ambulance Driver, Brookwood, Surrey

(4)

Our echoes roll from soul to soul

Alfred Lord Tennyson

Brookwood Military Cemetery
Surrey, England, November 13, 2000

Cedar, yew, and holly shelter Brookwood's carpet. In late autumn, viburnum, berries, and flowering shrub tint the green on green, and there are birds – blackbirds, thrushes, doves, and robins everywhere – keeping the faith. And in the early evening air, the fraternity of lives lived and snuffed in the flare of a match, convene in whispers of what might have been.

" Bird-song, " ventured Thoby Carlyle out loud, *make a perfect title…*

" Yes ! "

" Who…? " He'd been alone and self-absorbed for the last hour, blind to the entry of the young woman now standing at the elbow of his father's old bomber jacket.

" Sorry. Didn't mean to startle you. You read my mind – I mean, the silent graves, and up there, the *symphony…* " And for some time, the two intruders peered at the ruffling conifers that towered round the precinct, and listened.

" Yank, are you ? " Sarah was gone just a month, but the hair cropped about carved features, olive complexion, and stunningly vivid eyes hit Thoby hard.

" Canadian, " replied Marie patiently, for about the twentieth time in the last few days. But in this cloister far from Quebec, the label had acquired an abstract ring. Since gliding up the Solent, her geographical moorings had gone adrift. Even surrounded by hundreds of dead heroes, 'home' was a concept in flux.

" Oh dear. Apologies. Anything beyond Land's End defeats us. "

They'd hardly spoken, yet Thoby sensed a woman who had 'umph', a quality touted by his late grandmother, who'd risen from a marriage of forlorn rectitude during 1914-18 to pretty well 'umph' every Tommy on leave. In fact, Marie's sheer proximity verged on disruptive.

She was apparently indifferent whether he spoke again, quite poised, one comfortable in the limelight – the antithesis of Thoby's current agonizing notoriety. Here was his wife dead and professional world imploding, yet his pulse throbbed in the throes of infatuation. He should have been hiding in shame in the bushes. He ought to have looked down and walked away, but a cachet blew from her hair and Thoby looked straight at her.

" A relative then ? "

" My grandfather, " as if he'd just risen to join them, " my Mom's dad. Never knew him except in photos of course, but he looked handsome. I remember one of him in his flight gear; the eyes seemed frightened...perhaps he knew. He died at Dieppe right after that. Canada still mourns the disaster, but we never really held anyone to account, and just silently hate the English for it – guess I should blame the Germans too, eh ? They shot him down. "

Who said graveyards were desolate ?

Thoby exhaled audibly, self-recrimination dwarfed by another's loss, one which played in some discovery for this woman. And in that regard, he was then most bitterly attuned.

" I think he was flying a 'Hurricane'. He pancaked into the Channel, but his, his... "

" 'Canopy' ? " Thoby had seen enough films to make a guess.

" *C'est ça.* His canopy jammed on impact and he sank. A friend of Grandma's in the War Office told her they found him clutching his revolver. He tried to blast his way out... "

" Horrific... " For an instant, Thoby envied the hero's death, so clarion beside Sarah's needless end, or for that matter, his own life's work, squandered for the shilling of a tawdry 'science'.

" How lucky being born when we were... "

Lucky, but you can still lose it all in any era.

" You know, that indifferent rule of nature, no rhyme or reason, but here we are and there *they* are – ever read Thornton

Wilder ? Anyway, I'm not religious, not now anyway (ignoring the reflex lamentation of 20 nuns in Quebec City), but I suspect we don't completely leave the earth. In a way, I feel like I've just communicated, 'looked' into his cockpit and comforted him. "

Marie glanced at Thoby. Was he listening ? He looked distracted, in turmoil even. She noted the thatch of sandy hair, deep-set, cornflower eyes, and the lanky frame. A plausible stand-in for Nigel Havers, but time to end this. " I've gone on… "

" No, no. Not at all, not at all. A privilege to share revelations…*cathartic* really…for me, that is. Important to let the words out I'm finding these days. " *Enough about your wretched self, Carlyle.* " But which is your grandfather's…*ah.* "

Marie had pointed directly behind him. Thoby stepped carefully around the thin slab to read the inscription.

" 'Flight Lieutenant André de Billy Rioux'. Sounds distinguished – *but so he is !* My hat's off Miss, and England's too, I'm sure. "

" That's very kind. Thanks, on *his* behalf...guess that's two visitors more than he expected today, " and Marie unloaded a winsome smile which slew Thoby. She was in no hurry; in fact, she could have gone for some hot tea and a couple of Mme Bédard's scones, right there in the rows. A tableau formed briefly, of two iron chairs, and an endless line of ghostly young waiters. She poured a cup. " Tell me why *you*'ve come here – you're English aren't you ? " She realized neither of them had moved for some time; they seemed rooted to the spot.

" Indeed, yes. Well, ah... " Guilt surged through Thoby, making his eyes water: his father's son, standing at his father's feet. Christ, his own life spanned twice that of lads buried there, and what did he have to show for it: public revulsion, a childless marriage buried with his wife's excruciating death. No pilgrims would beat a path to *his* grave. His heels began to rock unsteadily, until an instinct said keep talking; this woman could be a lifeline to sanity.

" My father loved art, was an excellent water-colourist actually. I have one of his early ones – *stupid* ! They'll *always* be 'early' won't they. He left school at 16 to paint and worked at an art shop somewhere on the King's Road in London, then suddenly beetled off to your Rockies in the spring of 1939. He'd seen these prints of vast mountains and prairies and had to go and paint them for himself. When war broke out, he was 18 and somewhere in Saka…Sa… "

" 'Sa-*skatch*-ewan' ". She wondered what he'd do with 'Chibougamou'. " It's tricky. "

" Right…so he walked into the first recruiting depot and joined the Canadian air force. Survived the Battle of Britain, moved to Bomber Command and flew 23 sorties into Germany – survived the 'whole show'. Only, it killed him... "

" It says, '*December 25, 1953*', " Marie prompted, respectfully.

" A Messerschmitt tagged his Wellington somewhere over Holland in 1943. He coaxed it back to Londonderry on one engine, but it disintegrated when he clipped the ridge above the landing tarmac – God knows why they put an airfield under a hill – the nose bounced clean off. He broke some bones but scarred his face and hands badly trying to free the 19 year-old tail gunner, who melted in front of his eyes. His entire crew perished. They said my father never got over it… ”

A nightingale chorused overhead, causing Marie to think of Quebec for the first time since sailing.

“ Christmas morning, 1953, my mother couldn’t find him. He’d put a diamond necklace and a rare edition of *Idylls of the King* under the tree, then gone out to the garage and ended years of guilt and depression. My mother was pregnant, and I arrived New Year’s day…his messmates lobbied to have him here with the others. ” Thoby didn’t add that he’d never been to the grave before.

Both stood quiet, absorbing their respective tales, eyes misted.

No, thought Marie, *this isn’t a place of death*: *I feel too alive here*. Restless heels had brought her, and now she’d found a stepping-stone, a path of sorts towards ‘family’ in England.

Her intellect stirred on an innocent query, as to why, of all his work, the *Idylls* had been chosen – though it *was* Marie’s favourite photographer and Victorian whirlwind, Julia Margaret

Cameron, who’d slaved to illustrate them for Lord Alfred, her bosom friend. Marie rummaged for a suitable line. She leaned forward and clasped Thoby’s hand in both of her’s.

“ On my way now, but today’s been very special, for both of us I think. We’ve seen ‘*glimpses of forgotten dreams*’ . ”

Thoby, rescued from the irretrievable, was flustered.

" Heavens, you know your Tennyson... " awkwardly bowing goodbye. He could only watch as the tight jeans, black turtleneck, and fitted leather jacket glided gracefully away.

He was left pondering whether he'd condemned himself to always looking back...

Not wishing to appear the pathetic figure, Thoby moved a few yards north into the WWI section, but stopped abruptly at what his Brookwood Guide listed as 'Plot III, Row I, Grave 16' .

" Hello...*Hallo, Miss !* Look at *this* one ! " He heard his voice carom round the outdoor chamber.

Marie turned. Since they were alone, she had to be the one summoned. She strolled back good-naturedly, with a quizzical smile. Had the experience proved too much and he was now going to unravel in front of her ? Conversely, what had he discovered ? What else here could affect her; no other 'Rioux' spirits lurked, surely.

All the same, her interest was piqued by the fresh-cut flowers laid up against the marker indicated.

" Forgive my yelling, " Thoby began, " but here I am tramping along thinking 'all these young men', then here... "

Marie dutifully read aloud the inscription below the engraved maple leaf:

" Lilian Beatrice Nichols
Ambulance Driver, C.A.S.C.
March 1, 1919
Age 18 years "

and, after lifting the bouquet at the base of the stone, the dictum partly obscured by encroaching moss and scrub:

“ ***You are not dead, just gone away,***
I love you as in yesterday ”

Her eyes welled. You had to be without a pulse not to wonder.

Husband ? Unlikely, at that age. Brother, father, first love, blown to bits ? Flung herself into the cause to dull the pain and ‘carry on’? Skilled driver literally the quickest route for a woman to the front, then died herself, carting back the wounded ?

But how to explain the date, *post*-Armistice. What was the story ?

And the flowers – Marie would never forget, because they were delphiniums, out of season, lush and supremely blue – were they tokens from another Sister who made it into the new century, an aged beau still rubbing a tattered photo in a ‘home’ somewhere, a niece or grandnephew on a pilgrimage like Marie ? Or was it a ritual, founded by a local family touched by ‘that Canadian girl’ in a distant sojourn ?

Thoby kept mum while Marie mulled over the record; just her returning fanned his spirits.

“ I must say the name’s quite English…but what of it, she *is* with the Canadians. ”

“ *C’est bien curieux…* ” A frisson ran down Marie’s neck. “ Think we were meant to see this – sorry, I should ask your name ? ”

" Carlyle, *Thoby* Carlyle. "

Marie laughed, at the same time backing away and ending the client interview. " 'Thoby' – now *that's* 'quite English' ! "

She shook his hand briskly and was off again before Thoby realized he'd forgotten to ask her's. Despite valiant effort, he'd been unable to recall any Tennyson to match the occasion and had to fall back on Rupert Brooke, '*And is there honey still for tea ?*', but decided that was too cute, and so lost the opportunity to invite her somewhere. As she retreated through the long shadow of the Cross of Sacrifice, he thought of Sarah gasping in her huge leather chair, and blurted after her, " Do you smoke ? "

Without turning, Marie trilled back, " No. Thanks. "

" Good ! Tha…that's brilliant, " Thoby spluttered to the hushed troops.

(5)

'Wooten House', near Woking
November 15, 2000

Neale slouched over the withy fence to ogle the estate. The classic 'Surrey brick' manor reposed on a descending lane mantled in giant oaks, vines, hedges, and crawling ivy; small winter flowers burst everywhere like corsages on a thousand formal guests. Casement windows and clever terraces gazed in all directions. The western prospect framed a soft hill dotted with deer, sheep, and an upward-marching line of those bushy, ice cream-cone trees Neale often saw in children's stories – when, wired to favourite arias, he prowled the book-sellers, thumbing for the innocence which had eluded every stage of his life.

It took only seconds to form a gut dislike for his new quarry: why would he do anything to forfeit digs like these ?

Neale pushed himself away from the fence in disgust and plodded up the lane to the adjacent property, where he passed directly under the yew arch to a thatched portal and yanked the antique bell cord.

A sharp little creature, an escapee from Dickens who might well have answered to 'Mrs. Treadmill', peered round the great door.

" Good afternoon, have you seen Mr. Carlyle today ? Perhaps he left a message for any visitors ? "

" Mr. Carlyle ? "

" *Thoby* Carlyle, yes. Your neighbour isn't he ? "

" And who might be asking ? "

" A colleague from work…supposed to meet half an hour ago. "

" British Andorra, of course – oh my, there's quite the furor with you lot. "

" Um, yes, unfortunate…but Thoby ? "

" Well now, I imagine the dear man is lost these days – since his wife's death you know. Not surprised he's forgotten something, just look at his garden. I did see him at about half eleven this morning at the chemist's…he said something about going to 'the cemetery' later this afternoon. "

" Thank you madam, sorry I disturbed you. "

Neale turned and set his course for the local churchyard.

" Who should I say called ? " the Treadmill warbled after him.

" Bertie Wagner. "

**

" *Merde !* "

Neale grumbled in the shade of a Saxon tower. Two chilly hours had dragged by and the offending widower had failed to cross his sight-line on the polished marble twenty yards away; nor did it seem likely that he would now, given the sun's rapid descent. He felt as frigid as the surrounding Crusaders, landed gentry, spinsters and Baronets galore 'of this parish', not to mention the centuries of barristers and infants carried off by plague, pox, or typhoid. Most of these, he noted, were 'Sacred to the memory' of those themselves long forgotten.

He must have read the inscription a 100 times in the past hour:

CARLYLE, Sarah Anne Donohue, Beloved spouse of Thoby Carlyle,
b. November 22, 1963, d. October 13, 2000

It was 4:30 p.m., his regularly appointed hour, but Neale had nothing of value to report except the bizarre death of Roger Herschel in Saturday's train wreck – and that only if his principal hadn't seen the telly or the papers.

His mobile felt as cold as the present company as he punched in the residence number.

" Prinsep. "

" Mr. Prinsep, I' m afraid I haven't… "

" *Neale !* For God's sake man, why are you calling me right now – *Christ* you're the devious one, using the rails ! " His admiration was fleeting. " You bloody well lie low. This'll rattle Carlyle. He'll be more inclined to talk reason. Otherwise…but *don't* call me or the group for at least a fortnight. "

" But I really… "

" Be *gone* Neale, you give me the creeps, " and he rang off.

A thin smile crept over Neale's face. It felt warmer suddenly, and he could almost hear a round of applause lift from the yard. It was the nearest thing to respect he'd ever won from B.A., and he determined not to correct their false assumption.

Prinsep was evidently flustered. It was novel in their dynamic to have him soften on a deadline. Neale adjusted strategy accordingly.

It didn't escape his considerations that the U.K. opera season was imminent. With clever planning, Neale could hound his rabbit *and* indulge the finer things with minimal inconvenience. Whether he sold the scientist a bill of goods or merely offed him was irrelevant.

Neale regrouped directly in the cozy confines of the *Rat and Parrot* in Woking. After three pints of 'Bishop's Toe' and a full hour with B.A.'s dope sheet on Carlyle, he was satisfied. This Carlyle had to be feeling naked: wife dead, his partner-in-crime at B.A. tragically erased. Neale decided on little touches. Make him feel shadowed, uneasy. Maybe uproot him from that estate of his.

The first contact should be intimate and unnerving. All he needed was to find that punter at the London mortuary, the one whose off-track fetish bled his income. He owed Neale big-time for a kindly word with certain baddies in the east-end.

First though, a bruised professional curiosity demanded he learn where Carlyle had gone that afternoon.

(6)

Marie glanced idly at a copy of the *Sunday Telegraph* on the return trip to London.

'SALISBURY RAIL DISASTER : 3 Dead In Leaves On Track Horror' blared the headline. The victims included a local tobacco official recently embroiled in a 'whistleblower' scandal.

Reading the names drew Marie right back to the *Nichols* gravestone, which this time jostled her memory. The night before sailing, her mother had tucked a folder of some kind into her bag – 'might appeal to the detective in you dear' – adding something about 'threads for your English trip'. Much wine had been consumed, but her mother's voice repeating the name 'Nichols' hung distinctly, and now intriguingly, in her sudden recollection of that last evening.

At Woking, Marie changed for Waterloo, taking simple pleasure in making the connection, in being en route. She'd pared away contrived scenarios in her life, expanding possibilities. An afternoon in Brookwood played well, letting her soak up the melodrama of real history. She'd loved the solitude, the birds, and the wondering about past lives. Even the Englishman had been diverting, in his reticent, seemingly tortured state; but she quickly wrote off her sentiment as feeling indebted for the 'Nichols' discovery.

Marie stared out the window at the sunlight lifting from the passing bricks of Wimbledon, trying to imagine Lilian and her world of 1919. She pretended they'd been sisters and their bond would compel sharing what exactly had roused her to action.

His Majesty's recruiters would not have enticed neophyte girl-Samaritans, especially as ambulance drivers, a statistically dangerous function, and the data on Lilian's Brookwood stone suggested her service entry with the Canadian Army Service Corps couldn't have been much earlier than 1917. By that date, Marie reasoned, even back in Canada, she must have been aware of the decimated English schools, the 'widowed' country towns, and the men returning blind and limbless. Surely by 1917, when patriots battled growing crowds of 'conscies', and 'the common foe' defied meaningful description, Lilian hadn't risked all her tender years 'for King and country'.

No. It must have been something deeply personal, self-driven. Something she needed to prove, pure challenge perhaps, adventure – it wasn't an exclusive male gadfly, even then – plodding through shell and desolation to retrieve the human pieces, a saviour in her own guise. Or did she search for someone in particular in the maelstrom ?

Vauxhall whistled by, and Marie had to adjourn her inquiry at the spontaneous observation by a nondescript matron across the aisle.

" Did you know that some Bolshevik mandarin came by here just before the Revolution and noticed the 'Vauxhall' signs along the platform ? When he went back, every stop in Red Russia was labelled 'Vauxhall' because he thought it meant 'train station' ? "

Waterloo appeared almost directly. As she stepped down, avoiding the proffered arm of a young man in a Swedish hockey jersey, Marie drew an interim conclusion. Lilian had been a creature of some refinement, but not prisoner to the false dash and feathers of bygone eras; the hooves of the Light Brigade had not pounded under *her* window – an element of the wanderer, yes, but with practical, caring purpose. Much comfort Tennyson would have been to her in the gas-swill of Flanders…

Marie let out a healthy sigh, as if shedding a mantle, and turned thoughts to a light jog now along the Embankment, then a long dinner. Marita, her Norwegian host in an elegant Chelsea B&B, had urged Marie to try the *Cross Keys.* She'd take her mother's folder with her and continue the 'Nichols file' in the company of a good *Shiraz.*

**

Thoby lingered a full hour at Brookwood following Marie's departure. It had taken abject circumstance to get him there, and he might never be back.

How pathetic, seeking absolution from your dead father. But he was indisputably galvanized, groping towards a resurrection; if he could just make amends. As he passed the 'Nichols' plot on the way out, with its poignant bouquet, the scent recalled the young Canadian woman and their hushed exchange. Gone now, like an apparition...

Idiot ! You've been 'visited'. You were supposed to be here !

A glimmer of redemption lit Thoby's return down the station path. His body seemed to float along, led by a wreath spinning improbable scenarios: true romance, absolution, a child – for whom he'd survive no matter what his sins – and the woman, reappearing beside him, gesturing and smiling in that devastating way. So real her presence, Thoby, in a surge of gratitude, couldn't help turning and kissing her full on the mouth; then, quite alone again, blushing from shame and excitement.

A fierce laugh escaped as he stumbled on the truth that when you've nothing, absolutely *nothing* left to lose, at rock-bloody bottom, life can be ethereal.

**

Nothing walks with aimless feet

Tennyson

Thoby returned to Woking and boarded the next train, assuming it went to Waterloo, all the while dreading the thought of his empty house, a glaring testament to hubris. What ever was there to go back for ?

Easier to lose himself in London for a while. Find a concert or an outrageous revue. Take stock amongst the crowds in Covent Garden. Or better still, walk the entire Embankment, throwing back *Pimms* at every barge and dance bar until he reached the King's Head & Eight Bells, his father's old local. Who knew where he'd sleep ? He didn't much care, and for that matter, he wouldn't be alone: didn't Dickens used to haunt London through the dead of night, trekking out his guilty muse – in fact, wasn't he a frequent caller at Thoby's namesake on Cheyne Row? One never knew, the 'sage of Chelsea' might take them both in and offer wisdom. *Please sir, may I have some more…?*

So rapt was Thoby on the road to a new self that several stops shot by before two stimulating facts emerged: he *was* going to survive; and, the train he'd taken was bound for Portsmouth, not Waterloo. The latter revelation came as Guildford's Cathedral spire glittered loftily through the right window, and seconds later, when the River Wey dawdled off on the left.

The error sharpened his resolve, injecting tentative action with detail. He exited at Godalming, the next station, and proceeded on foot through the picturesque community, finding his pace quicken as the rampant affluence grew too familiar and accusatory.

He bent uphill and soon broke into lush, rolling country, content to let one public path fencing an estate lead him to another. He stopped once, involuntarily, on realizing he couldn't remember a time when he'd listened to evening birds or wind in the branches. But a vestige of boyhood leapt forward from his afternoon – David Balfour onto the broad highway – and his psyche whistled with clarity. Thoby could have legged it clear to Hadrian's Wall.

Physical and mental bearings began to align. Under the lip of a treed ridge to the west, Thoby spotted two pill-box emplacements, a stern admonition to Nazis invading from Portsmouth. They recalled the War, his father, and reaffirmed new goals.

Time to fire off a second salvo. A solitary red phone box appeared at the next crossroads, draped in wisteria: the very opportunity to verbalize, take action. He rang up Algie Pemberton, his solicitor, at home. Algie was his only confidant, apart from the young scribe at the *Times* who represented the other principal item on his brief to-do list, and a regular, visible visitor during Sarah's final weeks. He would cause little stir popping round to retrieve Thoby's laptop, mobile phone, assorted killer documents, two photos, and a grab-bag of clothes. He hadn't a clue where to have the stuff sent but that would sort itself out.

He was astounded at how easy it all was. He gave instructions to sell *Wooten* immediately, without listing or signage. Proceeds to go into his Swiss bank account – a useful perq to be rescued from his tenure at B.A.

Thoby rang off feeling upbeat: it was a start. There *was* going to be a future, and he embraced it with the verve afflicting recent converts. He quickly regained his pace. By the time he spied a row of Ms Potter's rabbits eying him from someone's vegetable garden, Thoby's retooling was underway, and a strategy was gelling. He gave it a typical B.A. moniker: *Project Turnaround*, tickled by the knowledge that Marketing would in his case name it *Turncoat*. Thus far, it consisted of:

Plan A - wreak irreversible havoc

Plan B - scatter to the four winds and play it from there

and, though too deferential to reduce her to an item, there was an undeniable itch to see the Canadian again.

Vespers pealed from a nearby church. The quaint intrusion of sound unleashed a flood of association, real and imagined: the choirmaster chiding Thoby for hurling snowballs at the girls from St. Barts; his wedding day; his father's stern admonition on the steps about something – *anything*, as he'd never heard his voice – or perhaps that was the male intoning in the pulse of the bells. Thoby could have sworn they were calling,

'Ellen... Terry... Ellen...'

He caught himself then, and paused against a great oak, rubbing his face reassuringly on the damp, tactile bark. For some reason, he felt mired in the 19th century, suspecting, as his mother's well-read lad, that it was due to his current plight, one drenched in personal melodrama, a fall from virtue, and now, God willing, a quest for something pure, something, dare he dream it, beautiful. So *Dickensian*, and hence his feverish pacing to shed the guilt. As if to validate his suspicion, Rudyard Kipling stared out through his famous specs at Thoby from a cedar shrub. But Thoby, imagination keeping even with his stride, saw the reverse parallel right away. Kipling's imperial trumpet had choked on Flanders mud; chastened and bereft, the scribe had died in a futile search for his fallen son. Looking over the fields to the surrounding hills, Thoby conceded that he had spent a subconscious life on the look-out for any nexus to his father, without, however, any attendant personal suffering, a fact which quickly stifled the enobling parallel. Kipling Jr. had perished in a purportedly glorious cause, at Loos, while it was others, his wife and legions of smokers, who'd paid for Thoby's enlistment in the ranks of industry.

The glow melting off the down ahead evoked another image, the gold figure on the Guildford steeple. *But why ?* Another visitation swelled Thoby's march.

His father's artistic idol had been G. F. Watts, the melancholy-faced sculptor and portrait maestro, crony of Lord Tennyson and, yes, of course, beguiled first husband of Ellen Terry.

Terry, whose radiant vivacity lit up the Victorian stage, not to mention Shaw and Tennyson, for over a quarter-century, had later resided on King's Road in Chelsea, mere doors from *Green & Stone*, the artist's shop where Carlyle senior toiled as a teenager.

In the '30s, years after she was gone, Thoby's father would often eat his lunch across from her home, doodling her face from shop prints of Watts paintings. A Watts repro had apparently graced his parents' front hallway, but his mother tore it down the day her husband killed himself. These tidbits she admitted accidently on Thoby's sixteenth birthday, and he'd begged her to dig out the print.

His mother refused to look at it when she found it, muttering, " Your father used to rave about her 'demonic virginity' …he always swore he was 'born too late'. "

The portrait at issue, '*Choosing*', hung permanently in Thoby's physical and mental collection. It smoldered with Terry's flaxen hair and tender pout, and in time totally seduced him – if only it were *his* face, and not the camellia, against hers. At a Cambridge cocktail, the budding scientist once happened on a coffee table volume of Julia Cameron photos and again gazed on the thespian *fatale*, this time resting her cheek against a papered wall, her neck and shoulders exposed to rekindle his fantasy.

It was the same naturally erotic charm which had penetrated the crumbled perimeter of Thoby's life that afternoon in the cemetery...

Not minding the hour, Thoby continued climbing, almost buoyantly, thoughts of London that night tossed now in favour of the Watts Gallery. He knew it lay ahead somewhere up on Compton Down, and a quick tour was plainly called for on a day strewn with emotional touchstones.

When Thoby hiked in off Compton Lane a short while later, up a slight incline past the Tea Room, he found a verdant close, robing itself in night. It could easily have been a BBC set for 'Darwin's Hobby Garden' or 'Sir Richard Burton's Tryst in the Arabian Ivy'.

He could still make out a low building, running perhaps thirty yards along the left edge of a large lawn, featuring numerous gables. Their great arched windows illuminated the sculpture and painting galleries christened by George Frederick Watts in 1904, his 88th and final year.

" Hullo then. "

A cheery voice wafted overhead where thick vines were attacking the casements. A Puckish figure of modest size, clad in a frayed tweed jacket, scarf, baggy flannels, and hair as tangled as his adversary, waved a pair of shears precariously from a wooden ladder.

" We're closed I'm afraid. Winter hours and all that...can I get you a brochure ? " As if there were some stacked handily in mid-air. " Always open for donations of course ! "

Cheery or not, a human sound from the dimming cloister jolted Thoby's train of thought.

" Ah, yes…to be sure. " Thoby looked vaguely upwards. " Silly of me. I had this notion – it's been quite a day – my father was an immense fan of Watts, you see, and after leaving the cemetery I needed to see what he saw… "

How do you tell someone, a total stranger, that you've recently accepted the likelihood of having hastened the death of thousands, millions even, lost everything that meant anything to you along the way, and only just stumbled on a faint, creative filament lighting the shadows round a hitherto invisible father, ditched your stately pile in Surrey, and…well, just wandered up here to keep the purge running ?

The voice in the sky descended, and its owner, revealing a mild limp, came over to greet Thoby, introducing himself as 'Richard, the curator'. His unaffected manner, and a certain kindred vitality, immediately engaged Thoby.

The curator was an accomplished student of his public. The visitor may have been a driven soul, a shattered son looking for answers, but he posed no threat, and, his mission evidently held artistic import. Formal hours could always yield to an opportunity for extending Watts' legacy !

" Let's say you're here by special appointment, shall we ? I'll tell Mia we're delaying dinner. "

Thoby began again, " That's extremely kind, but I shouldn't… "

But the curator waved him on, leading the way. Moving in unfamiliar shadows, Thoby balked for an instant as they dipped through a sunken garden and he came face to face with a pale, nude woman gazing softly at him over her shoulder from a bower of fig leaves. The curator turned.

" That's one of his *Clyties* – rather the best I think. "

It was too much for Thoby to have just stared for all the world at Ellen Terry in the flesh; the pose was so fluid and reminiscent, it was as if the Cameron photo had acquired three dimensions.

They entered the galleries proper through an enormous oak door and went directly down adjacent steps into a stone corridor which led into the sculpting cavern at the far end. Here, models for the historic works, *Tennyson* and *Physical Energy*, dominated the space. Several dummy heads of the former, with the poet's smoke-bagged eyes and fancy beard, eyed Thoby from divers angles, as if the Queen's Laureate were moaning, 'for God's sake, don't break *me* on these cold grey stones…'

In the passageway back to the stairs, there was a crisp head and shoulders sketch of Florence Nightingale – " the only one she allowed from life " his guide noted proudly – and another, of the Prince of Wales, done in the early 1860's just prior to his American tour, in which a callow, expectant figure gazed out, size and features cloned from the current heir.

The denizens of the principal gallery upstairs bustled in a world of dark tail-coats, virgin gowns and scarlet tunics. Their snow-apple flesh was untainted by *bain de soleil*, the hair pulled back from aquiline noses inflating noble brows; they were the Ancients, cavorting in the 'new' Britain, in high Victoriana. Three life-size oils in particular arrested Thoby's attention; the burning, coal-dark eyes of their subjects betrayed a common lineage.

" Just a few of the infamous Pattle sisters, Mr. Carlyle. With your name and their social zeal, I'm surprised they haven't leapt out and grabbed you for their salon. I'll bet you've run across Julia, if not by name, by product. Best-known and most prodigious of the lot. She's not hanging here, but she was a dour-looking one anyway...grandfather a page to Marie Antoinette, East Indian princess lurking in the tree somewhere…a relentless pursuer of 'beauty', and hence the 'Freshwater Circle' which she championed on the Isle of Wight. Her place there crawled with energy and eccentrics, people like Darwin, Lewis Carroll, Thomas Carlyle, Tennyson her neighbour, Ellen Terry the actress, and of course, George Watts. She waged war on them all with her camera, snapped them all for posterity – if sitting still seven minutes makes a 'snap' ! "

Probably all smoked like prairies on fire, mused Thoby bitterly.

" She obsessed in efforts to capture the mind and soul of her subjects – or should I say 'victims'. She was notorious for lying in wait for likely sitters; she once got on her knees to an unsuspecting gentleman visiting Freshwater, begging him to pose before learning it was Garibaldi. She called Watts 'Il Signor' and generally lavished on him, which between you and me may or may not account for that weary visage, but I *am* railing on aren't I... "

" It's fascinating, " ventured Thoby, sincerely, but apprehensive he might stop the rich flow by speaking at all. The cultural pantheon so casually referenced by the curator put his paltry affairs in their place and had a soothing effect.

" I guess she revered Watts as the *visual* side of Tennyson. I haven't agonized over it but I sometimes wonder if Julia may have fancied Lord Alfred beyond mere dulcet verse...what d'you think ? "

The curator looked like he was actually soliciting an opinion from Thoby, but ruminating on the foibles of such Victorian *cognoscenti* and whether they may have been a rhyming couplet had not formed part of Project Drag Green over the past decade. In the sorry march of years, Thoby had grown estranged from such whimsical revisionism, once the rabid stuff of Cambridge sherry hours – he made mental note to exhume his wit. Richard was underway again before Thoby could manufacture a reply.

" She married Charles Cameron you see, a man much older than she…hmm...you *do* know by the way she was Virginia Woolf's great-aunt – now *there* was a piece of work ! If I'd been Leonard, I might have shown her the path to the river quite a bit sooner… "

Richard finally caught the fatigue descending on the visitor. " Do you live nearby, or are you staying in the vicinity? You are most welcome tomorrow, and we can pick up again…? "

Thoby shivered violently as he realized he'd been wandering pretty close to that same 'river' himself until Brookwood. He searched the shining eyes of the curator, seemingly keen to regale at the drop of another hat, and he saw a beacon.

From that point, the voice filtering in seemed almost incidental, " …not taken a place for the night yet ? Well it's late, and we *are* blessed with an exotic out-building: horsehair cot, fireplace, breakfast tomorrow – early mind you – then you're on your own. Courtesy of old G.F.W. if you like…wonderful then. Follow me. "

And Thoby did, like a little boy to his room after a day at the circus. The building was warm and dry, musty like his father's old tool shed. He hardly noticed the murky forms and antique implements in their storage. He had enough energy to shake Richard's hand and thank him before his head hit the wool pillow like a ton of bricks. He remembered that it was garishly embroidered, '*Barra Boys Strutters - Lambeth Walk Follies 1937*'.

He fell asleep plotting his next move. He would call the *Times* fellow first thing in the a.m., unload the rest of the sickening tale.

Hm-hmm…Of arms and the man I'll sing, wherein I'll catch the conscience of the Filter King – inhale <u>*that*</u> *you bastards !*

(7)

November 16, 2000,
Portsmouth,
British Andorra Tobacco, CEC boardroom

" Ladies and gentlemen, Sir Geoffrey has joined us. This is an emergency meeting of the Chief Executive Committee. There will be no minutes. "

The Chairman, in a razored pinstripe and defiant red boutonnière, winced. On this Monday morning, he'd have preferred being trapped in an airless lift with a perpetual tape of Margaret Thatcher hawking Chilean wine.

The CFO forged ahead.

" As you must all be aware, Saturday's rail tragedy has, sadly, claimed one of our senior scientific colleagues. " At which several of the nine invitees rolled their eyes or stared more deeply into their cappuccinos. Hard seasoning in the field notwithstanding, they were amazed at the alacrity, not to mention deadly swath, with which recent CEC wishes had apparently been fulfilled. " At the same time, and as a consequence, one of the Committee's two most sensitive issues has been resolved. "

A smug smile or two and grim nodding all round. Sir Geoffrey coughed.

" And by 'resolved', I mean *totally.* Mr. Prinsep advises me that Dr. Herschel kept his family in the dark prior to his unfortunate approach to the media and they were shocked by his initiative; accordingly, only minimal steps had to be taken to ensure no B.A. documents remained at his residence or otherwise accessible. "

" A positive glimmer, " scowled the Chairman.

Silence reigned at the great rosewood table for several minutes.

" Dealing with the *outstanding* issue then, our information – again from the excellent sources of Damian Prinsep – is that Dr. C. is chastened by events and could well reconsider his position. I've asked Prinsep to have his people explore a full range of persuasion over the next while. I'm sure you'll agree we already face enough bad press, so if the eventual outcome of this issue must be other than pleasant, it ought best to transpire after a measure of calm has replaced the current turbulence. " On Sunday, the CFO had wasted a perfectly fine roast beef dinner charting this measured course of action.

" For the next two weeks at least, no official should comment publicly on *any* aspect of the media revelations, let alone anything in anyway traceable to the Dr. C. issue. That said, it wouldn't hurt if you all frequented your various clubs and associations and let it be known, *sincerely*, how important *all* our research staff is, and how much their work is valued, *even when* expressed in a controversial manner – QED everyone, we fear nothing in the science, but remain naturally protective of corporate fidelity and team play, etc., etc. Now, the Chairman and I are open to comments… ”

“ Thanks much, Patrick, ” acknowledged Sir Geoffrey. “ Anyone…Adeline ? ”

“ ‘Misfortune breeds opportunity’ . Things appear under initial control; therefore, how do we exploit the immediate situation to divert the enemy ? ”

“ Spot on, madam, ” allowed the Chairman, inspired by the show of resilience. “ Perhaps a media salvo that confronts everything, concedes nil, but shows dignity and solicitude ? ”

“ Right, ” echoed the CFO. “ We come not to bury Judas, but to praise him. A release conveying deepest sympathy to the Herschel family, noting how such personal and professional loss transcends any internal corporate rancour, and, um… the international scientific community will surely miss his contributions and promise, *thus* emphasizing our association, as his employer, with the respected world of academe. ”

“ Brilliant, ” pronounced Sir Geoffrey ever hopefully. “ You'll get on that release then ? Have we finished ? ”

His CFO, as usual, was out ahead.

“ There is one significant unknown in our wait-and-see strategy. It entails Carlyle's access to areas beyond his mandate. He ballyhooed about *Project Drag Green*, but I have a nagging recollection he's acted as stand-in member on other delicate undertakings – off the top, anyone confirm or deny ? ”

The Coordinator for Latin America brand strategy reflected out loud. “ He co-chaired our marketing group for about six months in the early 90’s, when Emile Fuentes was ill. Awfully young then, but proved a quick study on local trade and cartel issues… ”

“ Jesus, ” muttered the CFO.

“ I suspect Jesus doesn’t share our corporate mission, Patrick, ” the Chairman cracked.

“ …then he’s seen the transit maps and knows our *contrabandistas.* ”

“ If we’re talking Latin America, Caribbean… ” With some trepidation, Smythe-Jones, Audit & Security chief, waded in. “ there’s every chance he met the Iran-Miami weapons crowd – God, now I think of it, wasn’t he seconded to the NBG in’ 95 as ‘research’ cover for the Irish joint venture ? ”

Two other mouthes fell duly ajar, as if poised to exhume further horrors.

“ Let’s *not* panic, ” inveighed the Chairman. “ We’ll follow Patrick’s admirable approach, but every unit will do a thorough scan of *every* bleeding minute of Carlyle’s life here, and then cross-check with document inventory. If there’s an odour, we can revisit our moratorium. Remember, he’s only dropped a tactical device so far; could be that’s the limit of his arsenal… ”

“ Thank you everyone, ” said the CFO, imposing closure, “ and special thanks, Sir Geoffrey…next meeting TBA on short notice. ”

The Chairman wheeled himself quickly out a side exit from the long ante-chamber, directing the driver of his Silver Cloud to the *Athenaeum*, and a double, no, triple Lagavulin.

**

'Wooten House', Surrey
November 17

Algie Pemberton's dashing in and out of Thoby's manse did not go unnoticed. Not by the vigilant Mrs. Trundle.

The poor man hadn't been home in ages – probably bogged down in estate matters, or just avoiding painful memories – and she was all for popping by to see what was what exactly. Her inclination was to slip over after the dark-suited man in the sporty convertible had left. She'd made proper note of him twice in the past three days, carting off various items and folders; though she had to admit having seen him with Mr. C. quite often just before Mrs. C. passed away. Perhaps nothing was amiss. After some to-ing and fro-ing, she reluctantly tethered her neighbour's duty for the evening.

At 6:00 a.m. the next morning, however, that oily man from British Andorra who'd rung her door the other day came and went suspiciously after unloading a large bulky object from a van. Whatever it was remained in the Carlyles' front circle. Testing her patience.

At 7:15 a.m. – or so Mrs. Trundle later fudged it to DCI Lewis – she felt absolutely bound to investigate, and proceeded up the lane to do so.

She found no one inside the gate. There wasn't a sound about the place, not even of birds, which struck the good woman as odd. What she did see was a shaft of sun, pointing the way if you didn't mind, trickling across the dewy lawn and ribboned over a very spiffy pram parked at the Carlyle's entrance. It was the object she'd noticed alright, midnight blue, with the hood pulled up.

She was all-atwitter. A foundling ? But why showing up then ? Who besides herself cared about such things anymore ? These *were* strange times though, and that 'Bertie' character was definitely of the swarthy persuasion. British Andorra *was* under wide public scrutiny – land sakes ! Not a *bomb* in that thing ? And she leapt back involuntarily.

Get a hold of yourself Vera, you've been reading too much Ruth Rendall !

Her gumption returned when she spied the perfectly darling antique lace bonnet peaking from the fringe of a pink comforter. Her creased lips already formed an approving 'Coo !' as she pulled back the blanket and was met by something staring up at her, or more accurately, *through* her. A tiny waxen face, pea soup-yellow in complexion, with bluish tinges. The colourless eyes were gelatinous…

Mrs. Trundle hit the crushed brick driveway in a dead faint before she had time to discover the powder-blue envelope lying under the head. PC Thaw found it, and in keeping with the dainty scene, held the enclosed note in white gloves while reading it to the DCI. The message was computer-printed:

'childless in life
lifeless the child,
– are you missing your wife ?
you'll be with her soon
if you do anything wild'

**

Self-serving it may be, or perhaps just good policy, but when a portion of its inventory is clandestinely removed, a morgue in London seldom publishes the fact. Even when the missing item is an unclaimed, anonymous newborn, ravaged by jaundice and left in the loo of a pedestrian tea-room in Belgravia.

Mr. Carlyle's peculiar absence from his domicile, quickly and quietly sold soon afterwards, through a solicitor with no knowledge of his client's whereabouts save for the moment required to execute the transfer documents, didn't help. The Surrey Police were never able to satisfy their initial enquiries.

All in all, it was an extraordinary bewilderment which Mrs. Vera Trundle carried, unresolved, into her own grave.

Part II

The Slough of Despond

(8)

What a day-to-day affair life is.

Jules Laforgue

near Graf House, in the Ypres Salient
<u>November 5, 1917</u>

The observer peered without expectation through field glasses, careful not to draw any of the dreary light, dreaming vaguely of revenge. But his faith was now so savaged he could only muster a plea that the seasons, spring and summer, would reappear. And prevail, with green shoots, birds, and woodland zephyrs.

He wondered how his friend and tutor, 'Hopey'-Johnstone, would have styled the bleak chaos he surveyed. '*Object on the edge of landscape*', perhaps – assuming a 360° bog of carnal rot qualified as a scape – the 'object' being a solitary Lance Corporal squatted with his back against the east parapet of the forward trench. A Canuck presumably, shivering in his regimental kilt, busy prepping his kit.

The Englishman lowered his binoculars. As a brash romantic at the Somme, he'd flailed at the random pall of slaughter. The pall never lifted long enough to trust, so his creative will adapted. In and out of the formless days and numb months upon years, it rationed itself to fuel a ritualistic, often frantic probe of the wasteland for signs of anything inspirational, *any* evidence, however transient, of life still in progress.

In the other time, of poetic fire and bumming on the continent, life served an endless, sensual smorgasbord. The blur of horse and Landau crashing down the Strand, the sky-web of rigging along the Embankment, billowing here and there into glorious clouds of sail. An entire wall of Singer Sargent waiting his admiration at the Tate, or the painful wail of a drunken piper in Piccadilly late at night, or magically, the silky sway of a young woman's derriere as she crossed King's Road.

These were the clips that flashed sporadically in the evening star shells, the effervescence never heard at the front, where everything and everyone either shrieked, or made a violent sucking noise as they were swallowed by the ooze. 'Culture' was what developed on untended corpses, and not some pleasant land one fantasized returning to.

And yet, his one-man offensive had won some ground. Searching, scouring the ruination, visually keeping faith. In the long haul, his dedication had achieved more than bully beef or roasted trench rat.

Just days ago, he'd found himself abstracting actual colour from the morass: fine marble from the moonlit skin, rich blue from the *poilu*'s trousers sticking from the sunken pillbox. This therapy emerged after letting a Welsh chaplain convince him there was no need to rationalize the horror, just confront it. Days later, scanning the detritus, the logic hit him. Banking on Life's return, and accepting, until that sunny day, Death as a constant caller, you had to greet it *genuinely*. That was the only real choice; acquaint yourself without despairing, prepare resolutely, as if moving on.

By November 5, eve of the final storm in a lunatic 'campaign', he'd reduced his new wisdom to a metaphor, the conjunction of death and spring, which seemed brutally apt as he raised his glasses for a second sweep, catching the Canuck again, young and animate against the background of melancholy porridge. Which path would *he* be taking tomorrow ? Even assuming the best, how slippery the foothold on the living path, how far to go from this non-world before regaining the seasons !

Words, long dormant on the endless acres of mouthes, formed abruptly on the tongue of Captain Edward Fitzgerald Brenan, 5th Gloucesters. He fumbled in his tunic for a pencil stub and dispatch pad. Like a five year-old intently scratching out his name, he printed, '*We are closer to the ants than to the butterflies.*'

To convey the passion of existence with austerity had been a cherished craft, and he damn-near exulted at this little gem. The thirst for expression grew unquenchable. He remembered there was 'poetry', but could he call up any ? Something for the moment, by Laforgue preferably, his French idol; and slowly, a fragment trickled back, being free verse and peculiar…

Que l'autan, que l'autan
Effiloche les savates que le Temps se tricote !
C'est la saison, oh, déchirements ! c'est la saison !
Tous les ans, tous les ans,
J'essaierai en choeur d'en donner la note

It was now evening, as determined simply by the looming, smoke-strewn sky turning even darker, and the Captain continued to feel amazed. Oh to have shared his triumph in the mud with a kindred soul, huddled for a few exotic moments in the awful silence which screamed before a major putsche. But there was no one.

Brenan shuffled towards the end of the traverse trench. A quick final sweep from the forward line parapet and he could file his report with Staff – an entirely redundant procedure in his view, as only those lunching off china could fail to see after three months of torrential rain and barrage what 300,000 allied casualties had already learned.

Moving down the winding slit, he heard someone singing: it had to be the Canuck.

" V'la le bon vent
V'la le joli vent... "

He could see him as he came round the final bend, still crouched. He looked pathetically callow – Brenan himself being an ancient 23 – though not as young as some of the terrified Boche they were hauling in lately on night raids.

" Alors, vous êtes canadien-français ? "

His thighs ached with the constant chill, but Corporal Hébert sprang to attention with a clatter of equipment. Brenan waved off the salute and extended his hand.

Tabarnak ! An Imperial officer not only speaking to a colonial NCO, but shaking his hand. And no pickle showing from any orifice. Too bad his girl-friend and family couldn't see him now.

" Oui, Capitaine. Je viens de Lévis, tout près de Québec. "

Brenan recognized the insignia of the 42nd Royal Highlanders and smiled. A tartan singing a Gallic tune was par for the course.

" C'est tellement tranquille, n'est-ce pas ? J'espère que ça vous gêne pas si je parle un peu… "

Politesse, même ! Qu'est-ce qui m'arrive ? Every man he'd called 'copain', except his Sergeant, had been killed the previous day at tea-break by a rogue concussion shell from British guns. As if he needed further isolation to dwell on it, his keen eyes and ears had just earned Joseph night-watch at the riskiest forward listening post in the entire salient – *please, talk all you want !*

" Mais non de tout, Capitaine, je vous en prie. Ça me pique aussi, la silence… "

Brenan could not contain himself.

" Je viens de regarder le déluge-là, et il me vint subitement à l'idée que nous sommes tous prisonniers des entrailles de la terre. Qu'en pensez-vous ? "

" C'est ça, " Joseph answered rotely, less captured by the image than by the fact he happened to be staring at a German boot protruding from the opposite trench wall as the Captain spoke.

Joseph had more than survived his blooding at Vimy – he'd apparently 'distinguished' himself – only to be shunted into what became the 'Third Battle of Ypres' back in June, a few centuries ago. Anzacs, Tommies, and Canucks called it 'Passchendaele', though current patrols reported there was no village left to occupy.

A month shy of his eighteenth birthday, Joseph had brushed into pretty well everything up the line. When one million pounds of emmonal in nineteen mines blew Messines Ridge sky-high on June 7 to launch the whole nightmare, he'd shut his eyes when he felt a thick rain on his face, soon realizing it was chunks of falling flesh – 20,000 Boche killed or mangled in one sappers' blow.

Junior officers had come and gone like pop-up targets in an arcade. There was their latest subaltern, standing on the trench lip, his mouth a bubbling blister, his eyelids fused shut, silently waving them on with his revolver while drowning in his own fluids, too keen for the fray to have strapped on his gas mask.

And the CSM who'd gradually exchanged blood for alcohol to charge his veins and dull the memory. Not a single man remained alive in his company from Salisbury Plain. One clear night, he noisily mounted the viewing port and lit three fags in a row before a sniper's bullet took him in the chest – and his silver flask. They carted him off to Étaples, hysterical.

He was no philosopher, but the young Canadian was flattered. Here was this *officier sympathique* cruising the fringe of absolutely fucking nowhere, analysing the horror in someone else's language, and he wanted *Joseph's* opinion ! He wished, in fact, momentarily prayed, he could formulate one.

He fixed on the reference to 'the earth' and from somewhere in the sea of slime, gas, blood, and dead friends – even the Fritzie permanently mining the wall in front of him – the most poetic thing Joseph ever heard floated out. Its gentle, sacramental tone unnerved him.

" Pour que la terre leur soit légère… "

For an instant, the quiet lost its jangle. Brenan had no rejoinder; nor would he have ventured one. He was astounded. A million 'Amens' filled the air as this lamb said it all.

The two men groped for further commonality. Brenan volunteered that he'd seen pictures of Quebec's 'magnifique' Citadel and the St. Lawrence below, confiding that *his* sentimental cliffs stood at Freshwater, at the west end of Wight; the Corporal should really try and visit there on his next furlough. But the epiphany had passed, and Brenan chose to seal it with a written memorial, then press on, in case…

Out came the pad again. On it he printed neatly, in English:

'To commemorate reflections with a fine Canadian colleague,
in the slough at Passchendaele, November 5, 1917.

Gerald Brenan'

and then added hastily in long-hand below, as if Fate pounded at the door:

'Into the valley they rode, and rode, and rode…'

He proffered the rumpled sheet to Joseph, shook hands, then escaped along the duckboards before he might accidently learn the Corporal's name.

Joseph proudly read and re-read the 'colleague' part, but faltered on the rest. After awhile, he folded the note three times and buttoned it into his breast pocket.

**

When the first star-shell of the night flooded no-man's land, the corporal automatically devoured every topographical detail, immediately looking back to his own lines to check the degree of their exposure as well. To his astonishment, a huge, pear-shaped male stood a mere six feet behind him, lit up like a startled burglar.

In the same instant, he lunged backwards to push the new arrival from enemy sights and was amazed to see the oak-leaf collar of a General. And at his extreme forward post ! Brass typically showed at *rear*-line parades after huge losses to promote further sacrifice…Whatever the motive, Joseph had a visitor of rank for the second time in three hours. He wondered seriously if they weren't divine messengers, advance notice from God.

"Thank you Corporal," admitted the unruffled Corps Commander. "That was less than prudent of me. My ADC is forever knocking me down too." A young officer hovered, if one could do so horizontally, a few yards back in another half-frozen crater.

Star-shells were going up one after the other now, letting Joseph examine the intruder in a steady light. War was indeed a leveler, for here was a General pressed against his shoulder, hunched like himself in a tiny exposed pocket in no-man's land – though as pockets went, it was an architectural marvel, an impromptu redoubt formed in a shattered cemetery by three headstones of prior residents long since bodily evicted, and a French caisson blown fortuitously over and between the interstices.

Even hunched, the General cut a substantial figure, with a leader's aura. Yet his face was cherubic, his eyes soulful. Thanks to the lighting, Joseph recognized him from photos in the *Daily Herald*, towering over the English King whom he was escorting somewhere at the front. He couldn't remember his name, but knew he was admired by all ranks for meticulous preparation and a loathing of blind attrition.

" A lonely spot Corporal, hard duty I'm sure. Never think it's not valued... " Both men pulled their helmets tight and grimaced while a desultory German 'sausage' angled earthwards and exploded not fifty yards away. " ...or goes unnoticed, " the General swallowing the ironic timing. When the slop and debris had rearranged themselves, he asked, " How long have you been out here ? " His manner of speech was stiff, but Joseph read its sincerity.

" I' ave been fighting since March, sir. "

The big man's eyes glistened as the world lit up again. " Then you were with us at Vimy. "

“ Bien sûr, Général. ”

“ Glad to see you in one piece. Do your best to stay that way. I bet there are young women counting on your safe return. ” *This to a flea marooned under a thousand hammers !* “ Keep your head down for their sake, son – *you* don’t need an ADC to remind you ! ”

The General rose to an awkward squat and saluted; he’d never send a man anywhere he wouldn’t go himself. Joseph was too astounded to reply.

“ Good night Corporal, God speed. ”

Lewis-gun fire opened up and rippled briefly further down the Canadian lines – *don’t forget tomorrow morning gentlemen…*

The General slid back to his Aide before the next ‘Very light’ burst, barely able to see through tears of disgust. *This bloody mess ! Teenagers everywhere !* He’d risked his command by entreating Haig to stall a rain-sodden advance on a dubious objective. Weather had improved slightly in the interim.

For that much at least, Sir Arthur Currie was grateful.

(9)

January 5, 1917
Haslemere, Surrey

" Don't go ! Oh my darling girl ! Your home, your studies. You…you can't just…flounce off to the war. "

Lilian had determined otherwise, early in her seventeenth year, armed with the knowledge her mother had done exactly the same thing during the South African War.

" It's not a whim, mother. The university's been ravaged. I've seen boys from school – gone out and never come back, or sent home burnt, mutilated – I get so upset and I keep asking how we can help them. I have no father… "

Char bit her lip, stung by what followed as well.

" …or brother to enlist. Or even to be a *conscie* for that matter, and I couldn't *bear* being a 'land girl', hoeing veggies for the men. I've been a volunteer at the hospital for the last two vacs now, Mum. I speak perfect French, and I can *drive* for goodness sake ! "

It was bigger than that. No one could have faulted her mother's daughter for feeling frustrated by the turmoil – as so many women of the young century – how could she sit idly by and not participate in what was consuming the entire world ?

" I'll be a *driver*. You've heard everything Elsie Inglis, Cicely Hamilton, and all the suffrage people have said, and... and *done* ! It's important for *so* many reasons – and no fear Mum, romance with a uniform isn't one of them. I don't intend to collect bodies just so they can be refitted and destroyed all over again. I want to *preserve*, even if it's just a solitary soul. You did that for father didn't you... "

Char was speechless, limp with apprehension.

" Would you do differently now ? *No !* And you didn't then Mum, and I shan't either. "

**

Ypres salient,
north-east of Gravenstafel,
<u>7:15 a.m., November 6, 1917</u>

Without blinking, the driver swerved to avoid a dray horse, sprawled and eviscerated dead-center on the road, then skidded to a perfect halt between two jagged shell-holes.

" Let's have your *Ordre de Mouvement,* " muttered the young Tommy before raising his eyes. Then his jaw dropped at seeing a female so far up the line. " But you're, you're a... "

" Of course I am... " Then added, as if all was perfectly reasonable in the circumstances, " there's no else right now and they need someone. I do this all the time, just farther back... "

The nervous sentry stood across from the Bellevue casualty clearing station, only a thousand yards from the now-sporadic bombardment. A heavy mist draped the air, lethal with drifting mustard gas and the Circus buzzing angrily overhead after the Canadians' dawn assault. Early reports had wounded filtering back from Goudberg,Vine Cottage, Mosselmarkt, and the ruins of Passchendaele. In the ordinary course, as much as war allows the ordinary, field ambulances would have immediately scrambled into Bellevue CCS to gather any redeemable souls carted in from advance dressing stations and aid posts in the quaint reaches of hell. The drivers wished in vain for night offensives, so they could edge in after dark and not draw fire from aircraft or artillery. At that daylight moment, however, only a few hundred yards up the road at Meetcheele, a driver would enter easy machine-gun range. The Tommy was flustered, smiled weakly, then looked quickly about for an officer, but saw none. He didn't think to simply bar the way.

" Begging your pardon Miss, but you really oughtn't to go any further. "

The driver's 'tin lid' – rescued weeks before from a sinking corpse – tilted wearily towards the British soldier. Auburn hair poked out below the rim, severely cropped and matted in mud-spray. Pale cheeks were splattered with blood, more muck, and, assumed the soldier, dried tears. The eyes, though blood-shot, were resolute, other-worldly in their fix. What remained of the sentry's will capitulated unconditionally.

"Very decent of you Private, but do let's keep this just between us. *Please ?*" There was the ghost of a smile in the words but not her lips.

It was 36 hours since Lilian had slept, and a self-appointed mission kept her at the wheel through daybreak, long after her night shift transporting wounded from other CCSs to various field hospitals. Reliable intel from all ranks of the wounded she conversed regularly with in her tangled routes had pointed to a major push, and a premonition literally summoned her all the way up the line this morning, where she knew many Canadian friends would need her.

A voice – she could have sworn it – whispered repeatedly that it was the reason, the very *hour*, for which she'd joined up. It would be the experience, the special *duty* in fact, Lilian had aggressively pursued without fully comprehending, since arrival in Flanders. She was not a voyeur of the gruesome, nor a silly meddler; and there was nothing of the political in her motive. Man or woman, she was proximate and party to events shattering the world order and she wanted to absorb and understand them first-hand.

Along the way to this morning, Lilian had acquired skill and trust by relentlessly, but subtly, pushing the bureaucratic envelope. She 'just filled in' when a male ambulance driver was wounded and no replacement was handy; she coyly cajoled superiors into delegating thankless tasks, into acceding to being 'spelled' when unquestionably fatigued and only too grateful for a reliable and charming substitute. But, pressing ever closer to being on the non-milk runs, closer to the front trenches and the commingled smells and morass of conflict.

And now this very dawn, the logistics matched her mission. There simply was no one else back at White Chateau, man or woman, able to drive, night *or* day. Two male ambulance drivers had been, unbelievably, snatched by the brass to convey two lightly wounded ADCs and several other British officers to a Paris hospital. Her superior was felled by sepsis and too weak to restrain her, and Nan, her 'big sister' from the Canadian Army Medical Corps, had taken a bullet through the lungs the evening before from a local farmer irate at pilfering refugees, and a bad shot.

Her papers were valid and there was no order prohibiting Red Cross vehicles beyond that point – it was just foolhardy – leaving the befuddled sentry to retire, smiling, almost sweetly. He wasn't sure whether pride or sadness made them comrades.

Lilian revved the Rolls Royce engine and the ambulance jolted forward.

The Tommy gazed for some time, a large tear caught on his cheek, as what looked for all the world like a swell dinky toy bounced off between the two dreary lines of relieving and relieved, then faded into the distance. What piqued a lad's fancy was the marking over the red cross on the canvas side panel:

'Gift from the children of Nova Scotia'

Young – am I still 'young'?

Lilian thought of the boy-soldier and herself as she drove off. Both in khaki, doing their 'bit'. It wasn't the pimply skin but the scar of longing in his eyes. *Young and old, young and the old.* Innocence fought for air under a mountain of discarded limbs and a flood of screams. Trite lines from the classroom tolled with monstrous reality. *The quick and the dead…*

Scant months ago, her mother had pulled every female string in Great Britain, until, to her abject surprise, the Scottish Women's Hospital Unit grabbed Lilian in March, trained her for five weeks in things medical, then shipped her off to the Red Cross in Corsica and five months as a VAD worker in the fever clinics. Along the way, she had survived two torpedo attacks, a bout of dysentery, and three attempted rapes.

In all this, height, exceptional poise, and a mastery of colloquial French – in that order – had combined to obscure her age. But it wasn't till September that she cheated protocol against sending women under 21 to France, when she volunteered to chauffeur visiting Canadian medical officers up from the port at Ajaccio. They were impressed: a skilled driver with medical experience *and* French could not be left basking in the Mediterranean; within a week, Lilian was in Paris, press-ganged from the Brits by the Canadian army…

The short haul from Bellevue to Meetcheele dislodged epic sentiments. From the first flush of resolve, to unspeakable tasks in the demi-monde of war, and now, despite the cumulative assault on one so young, a kind of re-consecration this morning as she edged from the pavie onto the mule track and the mournful terrain.

Ten seconds later, the earth yawned on her left, rose in imitation of a thick-plumed tree, towering lazily in the sky, then collapsed like a spent geyser and slammed its innards on the neighbourhood. The ambulance lifted a full two feet in the air and settled, miraculously, five yards off the track on a duck-board indent. The windscreen was completely shattered and Lilian stone-deaf for several minutes, but otherwise, she was very much alive, terrified, and on schedule. Lilian calmly stepped down from her seat. She found her bag of dressings, strung it over one shoulder, and moved forward smartly on foot into no-woman's land.

She had every confidence her appointed goal would present itself, and it did, through the acrid wreath of debris: a cluster of bodies fifty yards ahead. Some writhed, some lay still, though all held silent, as crying out was not done.

The second wave had obviously gone forward, as stretcher-bearers were taking a breather and smoking beside their first retrievals of the day. How Lilian had ached for them that autumn. Often they needed as many as eight to recover a single casualty from no-man's land, knee-deep in mud, tumbling their burden in agony into water-filled holes as they faltered under easy sniping. When they reached the ADS, mud routinely denied vehicle access and they had to hump their charge another kilometre to a clearing station.

There was a collective blankness, layered over that of sheer pain and post-trauma, as the men fought the realization that a young woman had just materialized in their midst.

" Look fellas, we've got a spotted angel… "

" Where's Ned and Reg ? Not bought it have they ? "

Lilian shook her head. " But I'm what you lads have for the moment... " her flesh crawled all over with the encasement she now felt in the grasp of total destruction.

" Excuse me Miss, I'm just stepping over here to shoot myself in the foot... "

" A stretcher never looked so good, eh, Frank ? "

Lilian didn't bite. She was well-used to banter and saw only relief at her presence. She hurried forward and bent over the little clutch of humanity just as she did every day back down the line. Most, where discernible, bore the insignia of the Toronto Regiment. The awkward silence grew more surreal with the addition of a teenaged girl, aglitter in glass shards and blood, choosing who would be transported immediately to the next station and the 'resuss' – for transfusion and a life-saving op – and thus, who would not. Life and death, and Lilian tried so hard not to engage their eyes or show any hesitation.

The bearers nodded agreement with her on three: a certain amputation, and two severe head wounds. She would take one more, as she quite believed it would be the one for whom she'd ventured here; but he hadn't 'shown', and she feared she would have to press on without him.

" That man, *that man there* ! "

A British officer in shockingly unsoiled attire skipped past the stretchers, waving his swagger stick. Others from the reserve Canadian battalion were already converging on the object of his bluster. Lilian marveled how a prig thought to tame the surrounding fury with such squawking.

It was a visibly disoriented youngster, a Lance Corporal from the 42nd, spewing foamy blood, his kilt and tunic well-ventilated by shrapnel. When he wasn't frothing, he kept sighing,

" Seigneur, oh, Seigneur !

His comrades were having the devil wresting something from his grip. With no revulsion, Lilian saw the something was a man's arm, the khaki sleeve intact and showing a sergeant's stripes. Gore wobbled from the shoulder seam.

The prig persisted.

" Where are you going Corporal ? Where's your company… who ordered you to retreat ? "

Without pause, Lilian leapt in to secure the man, using her back to deflect the imbecilic rant. For an instant, the two of them swayed indistinguishably in cloth and blood. Lilian's action prevented the Canadians simply bayoneting the Imperial officer.

" There now. Gently Lord. You're in safe hands. "

" This man's a deserter. He's… "

" He's going with *me* to the CCS; he's a 'multiple', God forgive you ! "

One of the men, betting on her nerve, slid a stretcher forward and Lilian let the anguished figure crumple. The officer shut up. A limited acuity advised not dueling with this creature; he was a leader of men, with no comprehension of females generally, or what folly had allowed this one anywhere near the Front.

" Corporal, " ignoring Lilian altogether, " this man is under arrest. Escort him and report back to me when he's been sorted out – is that clear ? "

" Sah ! " The sudden cough of a patrolling Sopwith hid the derisory tone.

The five bearers rose in unison and another handful of volunteers pitched in to transfer the chosen four the short distance to the ambulance. The designated Corporal tried to keep pace with Lilian, who strode ahead, intent on getting her mobile domain in order. By the time they stowed her prize on the hinged rack above the others, she had the engine running and some of the blast debris whisked out. She stole a few seconds to pack dressings on the larger of his gaping wounds, then moved off quickly to leave machine-gun range – herself, four casualties, the Corporal wedged beside her, and one bearer clinging to the rear step.

Almost immediately, her special cargo shrieked at the heavily pocked mule track. It was the drivers' irreconcilable bane: the rush to get serious ones under the surgeon's saving knife, and the instinct to prevent jostling those in agony. Lilian braked, a little too hard, tore into her bag again and extracted a huge, pre-loaded syringe. Twisting, she managed to lean back and plunge the needle into the boy's thigh; the morphine produced brief murmurs of " doucement, tout doucement ".

As they got under way, Lilian stated to no one in particular, " I've drawn the veil. "

The Corporal was profoundly grateful for the silence, breaking it only to entreat her, conspiratorily. " You'll do the right thing by him, won't you Miss ? "

**

At Bellevue, Lilian approached two medical orderlies she trusted while the stretcher-bearer and the Corporal smoked and lounged about. After ten minutes, she emerged from the transfusion tent with a blank look on her face.

" There wasn't any point Corporal; they couldn't bring him round; he…he just slipped away. " And added, " At least, without pain. "

The Corporal felt oddly relieved. Only for the damn 'report' did he bother asking to see the body. Lilian led him to the long row of covered forms behind the surgery, waiting their last removal, and pointed. At her gesture, an orderly moved to the head of one and deftly flicked a blanket corner to reveal the boyish, now-placid face.

The Corporal's lips drew tight and his head hung slightly. The poor fellow's number was up, that was all. He couldn't imagine this dedicated thing acting deviously after such a brazen scoop. He shouldered his Enfield, lit a Gauloise, then turned mechanically to begin the slog back up the line.

At least there wouldn't be any silly fucking court-martial.

**

As league after dying league the beautiful desolate land
Falls back from under the intolerable speed of an ambulance in retreat
On the Sacred dolorous way.

May Sinclair

What would her chums at South Hampstead School for Girls be doing battle with today, Lilian wondered out of the blue. Jane Austen, Hardy, Tennyson ? Some stupendous new scientific theory ? She'd never considered herself very apt with the latter, despite an intense early romance with medicine. Fatigue killed any smugness when it occurred that she'd probably saved more lives in France and Belgium than the whole of Harley Street combined in a lifetime.

School hadn't entered her thoughts for months now; this was simply what she did, what she assumed she would be doing until 'it' ended: sleepless nights, flirting with death – flirting with the lads only seemed to bring on death anyway – lugging out the salvageable, all the while trying to be simultaneously ruthless and gentle.

'*Ride a cock-horse to Banbury Cross, to see a fine lady upon a white horse…*'

The ditty bounced over and over from the wheels' rhythm into Lilian's mind. Childhood rhymes for sorry times, except *her* horse was plodding towards the French coast and the Canadian hospital at Étaples. And not because Étaples was that much safer. German aerial bombers obsessed over its bridge, periodically throwing Lilian into a dug-out to watch bits of patients and hospital staff litter the air before dropping in the nearby cemetery. It *was* 50 miles from Bellevue, however, and with luck, the banshee fop might lose track of her cargo, at least long enough to save him.

'Him' was French-Canadian. A rather 'cute' patois drifted up from behind her driver's seat to tell her so. The other passenger, Nan, was drugged and dozing croakily on the opposite rack, leaving the francophone to a disjointed soliloquy. Lilian herself chattered into the chill air.

What ever am I doing here ? At once breathtaking and sickening, each kilometer disconnected her further from the ground; in a litany of desecration, it was an adventure unlike any in *Girl's Own*. And her nerve astounded her. She'd all but robbed two 'lung' cases from the system and was ferrying them in broad daylight towards the Channel through the mingled hordes of Allied armies. It was selfish in a way, but she'd chosen to assert herself, to make these two *matter*: her bosom mentor in the Corps, and a boy she should rightly have been discouraging at a tea dance in another world. And in so choosing, she told herself, she was jamming her own spanner into the engines of war.

The frenchie could have no idea where or how he was, any more than when she had him stowed under wraps that morning – thank God he hadn't yelled out then. She swore friends at White Chateau to silence and promised to be back by supper, but no matter what, " these two are coming to Étaples, *bien sûr* ! ", and that was that. No one had the heart to deny the young woman popularly tagged as 'our Flo' .

At noon, Lilian made a tea-stop at St. Omer. It played like a moment frozen in time: he gazing pitifully from his stretcher, she standing at the back peering in, half-asleep; both acutely young in their grown-up roles. It was here that 'mon frère' – weren't they *all* brothers-in-arms, and something French seemed right – looked straight at her and spoke lucidly for about two minutes before sinking back into a semi-coma.

" Ah, mon frère, vous êtes éveillé. J'aimerais bien savoir votre nom. "

" C'est 'Caporal'…non, non…c'est 'Joseph'. "

" Et votre nom de famille…? "

Joseph struggled to get his left hand up to his breast pocket. Lilian scrambled in quickly to guide it, then undid the flap for him, but let him claw the contents out and push them towards her. Joseph smiled wanly, eyes flashing, as she unfolded the torn sheet of paper.

" '*Collègue*'– vous voyez ? Il m'estime… "

Lilian stared dutifully at the note, trying to look very impressed; she hadn't a clue what he meant.

" Vous voyez, n'est-ce pas ? "

" Ma foi, oui ! C'est merveilleux, *merveilleux* ! "

Joseph's candle flickered and he began a relentless slide. It took all he had to brush Lilian's hand away when she tried to return the paper.

“ Non, non…faut la donner à mon amie…à Constance, à Montreal. ” His lids fluttered, he fell silent for a spell, then whispered suddenly, “ ‘Hébert’. ”

“ Ah, son nom de famille…? ”

“ Non ma’amzelle, *le mien,* ” and he didn’t utter another intelligible sound while under Lilian’s care.

Driving off again, she swore when she got back to Surrey she’d track down the Vicar who preached all those Sundays of war’s ‘noble discipline’, and how the horror brought men ‘nearer to God’.

Peering over her shoulder, Lilian thought Joseph looked nearer to death, period.

**

No.1 Canadian General Hospital
<u>Étaples, France</u>

Acting Matron Dorothy Arabella Bradford whisked down the chateau’s grand stairway to the gravel circle, all vim and vigour, just as the driver killed her engine. The senior Nursing Sister was followed by faint traces of sweat, gangrene, blood, leather, tobacco and antiseptic.

“ What have you today, Lil ? ” Bradford sang out, in full knowledge the usual reply never carried pleasant news.

Lilian raised her head from the wheel, seeking alertness. Two ‘bluebirds’ – the affectionate term for the Sisters in their bright blue dresses and white veils – put down their tea mugs and hurried over to greet her. They were shocked at first to see Nan in her condition, but heartened by the prognosis; their reaction to the young man unnerved an already drained Lilian.

" Quite a looker he is, just a boy like so many of them – but *Lil* ! He's your *double* ! It could be *you* lying there, *really* ! "

Lilian blushed. Her cheeks burned for the instant that a father, a first kiss, springtime in Surrey, lambs on the hill and Scylla carpeting everything, swirled around her. She tried to focus on the hope a young life targeted and 'saved' would send a message.

Bradford, hearing she meant to turn back directly, made Lilian down a plate of hot ragout, crusty bread, and two cups of tea – having to pee kept one awake.

" Dotty... " Her eyes did all the pleading, " don't report me, don't let them get him. There's a snotty officer wants to have him shot, to kill him, *now*, after *everything*, and look at the shattered thing – judge him for what, for being a colonial I shouldn't doubt – oh please, not *this* one ! "

" Calm yourself, Lil. No fear, I'll skew it, right as rain. "

Another cry in the great storm. Still, Bradford's empathy was genuine, if bittersweet, having so far lost two brothers and a fiancé to the war. The dear girl had clearly worked beyond limits, but found something in the wreckage to protect. So risky that...

" Don't think me silly...I was, I don't know how to say it, 'guided' to him this morning. Since then, he's like a...well, he's *not* dying here, not if *we* do something. "

At the tea-stop, she'd snipped Joseph's tags and collar pins, and any other identifying insignia. She counted on his not being coherent for ages, and her ruse back at Bellevue could help gum things up.

Lilian finished eating, then went directly outside and climbed in behind the wheel.

Her two colleagues and Bradford waved brightly as the ambulance nosed onto the main road, serenaded from the chateau dining room by a chorus of German patients belting Christian hymns.

**

Bradford didn't forget her promise. She did, however, feel peckish after ensuring the 'chauffeur' – as the military labeled woman drivers so as to withhold full status – had downed some nourishment, and beetled back to the kitchen for some scones and a quick cuppa herself. It was during this interval, ten minutes at most, that Joseph lay on his stretcher in the chandeliered foyer under the watchful eye of Archie Bramwell, a reluctant medical orderly.

Bramwell hadn't had a notable war thus far. 'Nowt you'd call valour there' his father lamented quietly in the local. Rejected everywhere for the first year, he finally slipped into an East Yorkshire service battalion in 1915, a tradesman's outfit commonly known as 'T'Others', but was abruptly denied front-line duty when his burglary record surfaced. He was summarily re-posted, 'condemned' as he put it, to be a 'dumb shite puke-catcher'.

Grumbling was his mainstay, and he seized the opportunity to let Joseph have an earful about women in uniform. When the only response was a minor twitching, he proceeded to rifle the patient's tunic, relieving him of three perfectly good guineas which Bramwell correctly assessed were no longer needed.

Joseph stirred briefly with the rummaging in his pockets.

" Friends…my friends…42nd Batt… " and he spat out some blood and sank back into unconsciousness.

" Right. " Bramwell took it on himself to ring up the field station at White Chateau – duly labeled on the stretcher – as soon as that dyke Bradford came back. The least he could do was notify someone to let his mates know; after all, he'd 'paid' for the service.

Part III

Paul and Virginia

(10)

A great log fire hissed and crackled into the dank November night. You couldn't ignore its beckoning. Not in the heart of good old London, mere steps from Cheyne Row, where Dickens and Chopin clattered up to pay respects, the Thames twinkling at the bottom of the street, and the neighbourhood ghosts of Eliot, Swinburne and Rossetti hovering close; not in the Bohemian reaches of Chelsea. The grinning abbot, whose stone-carved, ham-hock legs straddled the hearth in *The Cross Keys*, clearly agreed.

Marie glided into the pub, carefree and invigorated. The front room brimmed with neophyte solicitors, estate agents, and Euro-entrepreneurs – legit and not-so – most sheathed in black, grey, or pinstripe. Pints of Stella, graceful goblets of Merlot, and tall G'n'Ts rose and fell on an evening tide of cell-phone and chatter. Upstairs, around the open balcony, young males in white shirts and flashy suspenders vigorously feted a bachelor's imminent demise.

Marie threaded her way into the crowded bar to rescue a hard cider, then curled herself up on a wood pew near the blaze. The cider quickly added another buzz to the day's glow and the conversation swirling by.

“ …told the agent ‘10,000 a month, it’s a *river* flat for God’s sake !’, and she says, ‘But the sheik’s only *in* town once a month’, and I said – I tell you Bunny, I was inspired, I could smell that villa in Spain – ‘that, or Tupaq’ll snap it up tomorrow’. She looked blank for a second then signed on the proverbial. I swear she thought *he* was another Arab zillionaire… ”

“ We’re quite proud Jen, it’s actually one of those that went over… ” The bench opposite – two women in stylish sweaters and chinos, yellow macks folded at the side – lauded the virtues of a vintage yacht purchase. “ Andrew says the three bullet holes in the hatch are worth the price alone… ”

Marie’s head swung round. An afternoon at Brookwood had primed her to recognize the reference to Dunkirk.

“ …but you live in Guildford, where will you moor…? ”

“ Right here, at the east end, near Canada Gate – it’s brilliant, save us a packet when we stay up for the night or weekends – and in the vac, well, just hours to France, then work our way up the coast to Étaples or Belgium… ”

The next snippet sent Marie into the courtyard restaurant and her Shiraz.

“ Well, the *fête de vendange* is to *die* for. Stuff gushing from every fountain in Neuchâtel – Kevin and I never swallowed so much vino…you *must* come next year. ”

Minutes later, Marie was seated under an indoor palm, raising her first glass. ‘To Lilian, the ambulance driver’, a silent toast which caused a genuine tingle. Even then, her mother’s folder sat unopened across from her. Where it stayed, until a succulent medallions of duck had nearly vanished and a third glass stood ready. There was no hurry; Marie luxuriated in her independence, surrounded by the hum of life in another country, shedding or retreating at whim into the vagabond's unique state of grace.

Marie eyed the folder, speculating on its contents: would she meet a despicable family skeleton, or possibly fail to make sense of the contents at all, or…*but of course*, her aim should be to demystify the 'Nichols' reference. Her honoured 'guest' deserved that effort.

A frayed pink ribbon bound the satin leather, which had a simple gold 'R' etched in one corner. A piece of string held a tag to the ribbon. In a careful-looking hand, it read: '*Andrée's grandfather, great-aunt and great-grandmother*' .

Marie pulled the ribbon and spread the flaps. A faint mustiness blended with the perfume from her wine. There were several pieces of correspondence and at least two envelopes, the larger one apparently containing items other than paper. Marie pushed aside her coffee to sort things chronologically, which wasn't easy as not everything was dated.

Her waiter, a slender French youth, smiled when he noticed the array and scolded, " I regret Madame, *les séances* are not permitted. "

Marie started with the one addressed, '*M A. Mackenzie Rioux, 25 Route des Patriotes, Montreal, P.Q.*', bearing a George V stamp (she thought his nibs looked upbeat, though poignantly identical to his doomed cousin). The postage mark stood black and immutable:

'*7 VII' 17*'. It seemed odd that a letter from an 'Hébert' to a 'Rioux' should be in English, and flawed at that – though granted, the Montreal wing of her family had always been anglophone. The single page inside, possibly a sheet from an invoice pad, was embossed with a *fleur-de-lis* above a pair of crossed oars, and had a column down the right side.

Cher Monsieur Rioux,

We have been very much upset by your letter in May. We have received no news of our Joseph since January. Your daughter says he has left her with a baby to come and gone away to the war. We are not informed of this at all and we are wondering, does Joseph know this too?

You demand Joseph to do 'the right thing'– the Hébert family is honourable, and my grandson has no fear of a Montreal family. Joseph's père and grandpère died since many years and his mother went back to her England. She lived at 'Manor Cottage, Three Gates Lane, Haslemere,'. Her name is Charlotte Nichols. Maybe it is that you can learn something from her.

G. Hébert

The obvious pique continued in a follow-up note, envelope missing but this time dated, and signaling (Marie guessed) vindication. A rusty clip appended a separate, more expansive letter in a wholly different script.

5 octobre, 1917

Mr Rioux,

I am sending to you this letter.

You can see evidently our Joseph does not hide. We are hoping soon to embrace him here at Lévis. Without doubt, he will be writing to your Constance also.

Ghislaine Hébert

Marie held her next mouthful of wine before swallowing, letting the piquant fruit enhance consumption of 'this letter'.

PASSED BY CENSOR

21 septembre, Belgique

chère 'maman',

Comment va Lévis ! Je pense à toi très souvent.

Sans doute, tu devrais être très peinée parce que je me suis enrôlé pour la guerre. C'était dans un but intéressé, d'abandonner Lévis sans avoir t'averti, mais j'aurais pas pu passer toute ma vie sans voyager un peu. Je t'en prie, ne désespères pas, je suis sûr qu'un jour au futur, tu seras bien fière de moi !

Dans ces environs, nous 'les canadiens' sont renommés comme une force de frappe, et en consequence, les galonnards comptent toujours sur nous dans les situations critiques. Et puis les Boches, ils nous considèrent 'the ladies from hell'!

Je ne suis pas isolé. Depuis février, j'ai gagné beaucoup de nouvels amis – je suis connu comme 'Frenchie' (tout le monde ici a un sobriquet). En avril – au moment où la glace probablement quittait Lévis – nous avons pris une colline à Vimy. Est-ce qu'on a entendu en parler chez toi ? J'y étais blessé, mais n'aies pas peur, je vais tant mieux maintenant. Notre sergent me dis qu'il y aura peut-être une médaille pour moi – imagines ça ! Étant donné tout cela, je trouve que ces jours, je garde des sentiments vachement sympathiques vers le Canada.

À ce moment, nous sommes jetés dans une grande affaire. Si quelque chose m'arrivera, je te supplie d'informer <u>*Constance Rioux*</u> *à 'Westmount' (région Montréalaise – à cet instant je peux pas trouver son addresse) – elle est si belle, et connait très bien mes intentions sincères sur une vie ensemble.*

Penses doucement de moi.

Courage,
ton Joseph

Thus far, a bottle of wine, three espressos, and two liqueurs had guided Marie in velvet fashion through her dinner and 'readings' from the early shambles of the last century. She'd held off on the final envelope, much like a saved confection, because it was larger, blank, and gave no clues as to its bulky enclosures. Now she put her glass down and stopped fiddling with the green string figure-eighted about the two red paper buttons, and unwound it fully, letting the contents slide onto a clear corner of the table. This attracted curiosity from adjacent diners.

" The poor thing, Steve ! She's been jilted and now she's torturing herself with his gifts and letters. "

" Get a grip Judith...probably just mocking up things for a presentation... "

What slid out were two smaller envelopes, one pale pink, the other a grubby sepia, the latter holding the mystery objects. Both were addressed in different, though classically rounded female script. Marie opened the pink first. Its address had a modern ring: '*Aurelie Rioux, 25 Route des Patriotes, Westmount, P.Q.*' . When opened, a breath of potpourri escaped:

Haslemere, Surrey

March 10, 1919

Dear Mrs. Rioux,

It is far too late to beg forgiveness for not responding to yours of late 1917 – I was simply too devastated by its reference to my son – but common decency and circumstance dictate I write you now.

I had not seen Joseph since his infancy, and I suspect, will never see him again in this world. He would have been 17 when he enlisted, and undoubtedly passed through England on his way to France. And I knew nothing of any of it. I have written every Dominion military authority but no one has been able to trace his existence, except for a vague and 'unofficial' record of his death from wounds at Ypres. There was apparently a British officer's report at around the same time, urging some sort of charges against him, but that seems most contrary to the news of his possible decoration mentioned in your letter.

If only he'd known he had a mother waiting for him. He was so dreadfully young for such horrors, just like his father.

Here, there were several tiny smudge marks in the middle of the page, below which, rather than over, the text continued.

And now my dearest Lilian, Joseph's twin, has slipped away from me in London only days ago.

She served as an ambulance-driver in your army in France and Belgium – ironic I suppose, though I am so proud of her ! She was stricken with the influenza when she was being demobbed.

It has been altogether an unbearable year. The only will I find to write is fed by the memory of how poorly I was treated in Canada in similar circumstances long ago, and how, if Joseph has truly fathered a child there, anything at all about him should be shared not buried.

In that spirit, I have enclosed my last letter from Lilian – from quite some time ago I'm afraid. She never wrote again, or else her mail never got through before her return to England this month. Don't think me callous, I simply cannot bring myself to look at it any longer, and it may yield some solace for your family. It's all I can offer since she was never coherent from her return until her passing.

You will see from the various items, and Lil's own words, the awful glimpse of my children reunited, unknowing, on a hostile field. It is almost unspeakable, but such as it is, I let it speak for itself.

Yours very sincerely,

Charlotte Nichols

P.S. if there is a grandson or daughter, there will <u>always</u> be an English home to welcome either

---

Marie communed freely with the past, driven by a keen instinct for what she called the 'pure romance' of history. She was naturally attuned to the deeds of men and women, which for her, grounded the passage of Time. Conflict, challenge, love lost or gained, and above all, the random shreds of unsung players, pouring out their souls and leaving behind wounds and lessons. Marie teased friends for having a 'soap-dish attention span' towards the human current, and their obsession with living from a clean slate – 'life's so vapid if you don't poke around in the ashes !' Trans-Atlantic correspondence from WW1 sounding in the Edwardian period, then, captivated Marie. She reached for the second letter, realizing the packet for mailing the two envelopes must be gone, as the sepia note didn't fit in the first. She feared more sadness, an apprehension partly mollified by the fierce intuition of the adolescent author.

PASSED BY CENSOR

Ypres, December / January, 1918

Dear Mummy,

Happy New Year ! Are you at a party ? I hope so.

It's 12:03, and I suppose even here I ought to try to 'look back'– I know it's what one does, but all I see is heaps and heaps of bodies, so what's the use ? How grim and hollow the ring of the last bell left in Ypres tonight.

I know you didn't want me to go but I guess I had to, simply to discover why. I feel I've 'aged' a 1000 years, and it does seem eons since leaving England. I've seen what men have done to themselves and the world. We both share that now don't we – so much to talk about, and really, forget. Do I sound old and pathetic? It's everything to me that I am still your little girl, and survive in hopes you remember me that way – how often have I held a dying man crying to be held by <u>*his*</u> *mother.*

What I long for is tea and scones, and you rushing in with fresh berries !

Now that I've shut my eyes and ears a second, there is after all, one thing which I can claim as mine. It was early November, can't remember the date, or the weather – though it was surely wet and cold – well up the line at Passchendaele (the papers say the 'Third Battle of Ypres', a grand name for a horrid mess the men call the 'slough'). I remember doing my shift (driving the wounded) through the middle of the night, and then feeling suddenly refreshed, immune to danger, and something urging me out on a special mission – all I knew was I had to keep working and not fall asleep. I had this inkling there was going to be someone 'out there' in need of me. And there <u>*was*</u> *dear Mother.*

Some Canadians I know from the 42nd Black Watch were in on a big push that morning and their sector pulled me like a magnet. I felt creepy the whole time, but to make it short, I was nearly blown to pieces at the front when I snatched a young 'neuro' (they can't cope because of the constant shelling) from some absolutely insane officer before he could have the boy shot for 'retreating'– HOW SAD TO HAVE TO SAVE THEM FROM THEMSELVES !!

I tried to make it look as if the lad died on the way to the field hospital. He spoke once, earlier on, enough for me to learn he was French Canadian, but his condition made it unlikely he would speak again for some time. I stripped his collar dogs and other markings to make it hard to trace him, then I drove him right the way to the coast. I left him in safekeeping with my favourite sergeant.

It may have been wicked but I think it's my special bit in all this muck and I'm glad I did it. When I look at these scraps of identity, I couldn't give a feather for being 'mentioned in dispatches' by officers – these are my medals, and he was my 'p'tit gars'.

N.B. I couldn't fathom the piece of paper with the blood smear he pulled out to show me, but he seemed quite proud of it.

Marie put down the letter to examine the 'souvenirs'.

The most substantial was a pair of matching brass pins, about the size of a quarter, which she deduced were the 'collar dogs' mentioned. Each had the number '42' welded below a large 'C' – for 'Canada' she assumed – and one was dented. There were two swatches of soft cloth, one a dark green triangle, the other, square-shaped, of French gray. Marie had no idea what they signified but figured they were shoulder flashes. There was no blood-smeared piece of paper.

It felt eerie, handling personal effects from a violent passage, a sensation deepened by Marie's empathy with both players' longing to survive.

She recognized the dog tags right away: war films always had the officer cursing as he yanked the tags from the faithful corpse's neck. There were two of them, not really metal, but not wood either, a hardened textile perhaps, on two thin chains. Both were inscribed: *'Joseph G. Hébert, 42nd Royal Highlanders, C.E.F., 246 122'*

" See dear, there's the necklace he gave her. "

" You're completely daft… "

As if roughing out a new puzzle, Marie pondered the missing pieces. Clearly, there was a search of some sort for this Joseph, but why no further inquiry from Canada ? Was there lost correspondence, or had he returned eventually to Lévis and the family lowered a veil of silence ? What was the mother doing in England all those years – some sort of estrangement ? No one in Marie's family had ever spoken a word to her, good or ill, of any 'Héberts'.

And then there was the image of Lilian and Joseph out there, child-angel gathering the victim, and Marie's heart ached for the unanswerables. She returned to the letter.

I don't know what more to say, dear Mother. I'm still a baby yet I've thrown myself into a dark part of the world, and there are days and weeks go by when I don't utter a word. Some day I will travel everywhere and leave all this behind.

(Please keep these 'spoils of war' until my return)

all my love from a loveless place,

your Lil

Marie stared at the table.

Threads trailing into calamity, hearts long-silent, speaking. She tried to brush the cobwebs from the words patched across the linen. The background swelled with the passionate Euro hit, *Sogno,* agitating the spirits of the letters. Freed for an indeterminate furlough, they blew anxiously about, nudging Marie into action.

She carefully repacked the various items, paid her bill, lavishing gratitude on her waiter, then rose deliberately and proceeded to waft – or so it felt – out the doors of the *Cross Keys* into a gusty, star-splashed night.

Into a splendid though precarious infinity: it could have sucked her in right there. An emotional high carried Marie a full fifty metres before sailing her into a tall hedge – *the Great Wall of Chelsea !* She shrieked, bumbling along to the left until she found an opening where the Thames sent up a brackish teaser. The Albert Bridge, magically lit in the near distance, sparkled like a faerie span. Marie stood, wavering just a little, and gazed.

And she had a companion.

A male figure in frock coat sat above and to her immediate left, keeping the same view. Marie leaned gratefully against his pedestal for a moment before thinking she should introduce herself, especially when lamplight revealed the inscription.

" *Tabarnouche !* Such an *honour.* What should I say ? *Bien*...after all these years, does London still inspire you ? So much change...and *Mrs.*Carlyle – 'Jane', *n'est-ce pas* – is she content, nourished by your attention ? "

Very cheeky, Marie. But sudden intimacy with an intellectual titan, not to mention the wine, made her gush.

" Unearthly sky isn't it – *of course it's 'unearthly'!* – a thinker's sky I bet. *Delicious* air ! Good to escape your study. " Somewhere in university she'd seen an etching of the sky-lit attic where he forged his tomes.

The thinker couldn't disagree.

" I *do* have a confession, " Marie continued in a stage whisper, peering up at the chiseled features which marked one of the princes of Victorian iconography. " I never finished *The French Revolution*...or *Frederick the Great.* " She thought he looked miffed so added hastily, " But you *did* impress me, and...you looked veritably divine. "

She meant that, without feeling silly – not that she would have cared – but it occurred she might be 'sozzled', a terrific local term she'd overheard that evening.

" A kindred spirit, I see. "

A dowager, leashed to an Afghan of equal bearing, appeared like a rider from the shadows. " He's kept the view famously you know, been a perfect listener for years – but you're too young for such stuff my dear. You've loads of time to prattle like me later. It's getting on for midnight, scuttle off to bed now like a sweet child. "

Marie offered a fuzzy smile, and very nearly curtsied, but dog and woman had moved on, leaving the River, the cocktail barges sliding down the line, and the City lights vying with the stars. She glowed, she felt protective. For some reason, despite all her recent off-loading, Marie *cared* – though about what precisely, she was uncertain, other than it was a positive sentiment. She turned and patted the cold bronze feet.

Worth guarding, sir. Yes. Carry on. Then from her father's abandoned stash of 60's vinyl she heard her voice trumpet into the wind, " *All along the watchtower…* "

No reply. The front was still. Marie wheeled and swept up Cheyne Row, feeling wildly lyrical. Every corner in England seemed to trigger lines from somewhere. As she passed #24, Thomas' words rumbled gently across her path in what she imagined would be a Sean Connery voice : " *…not what I have but what I do is my kingdom* ". At #30, she turned the brass ring and flew up three flights to her room. Her clothes barely hit the floor before she was squirreled, naked, under the monster duvet, eyes shut to run a showcase of her day.

Life had been as rich as she'd hoped every hour since docking. Especially without e.mail and the ubiquitous need to be seen on the 'cutting edge'. What played on Marie's screen this night were the deep greens and rusts of Surrey, the moist land reeking around the moss and stones, and the parade of characters from her family past…

And tomorrow ? Research the letters as best she could, and then St. Paul's, numero uno on her London hit-list. With any luck, there'd be a fog so the dome would poke through like its heroic image in the flames of the Blitz.

She dropped off under the jets cruising into Heathrow and the amusing thought she'd encountered two men that day named Carlyle.

(11)

" Good morning, *Times* Health desk, Rose speaking. "

" Charles, uh, Somers-Cocks, please. " Neale had trouble getting the name off his tongue– *how does the guy introduce himself with a straight face ?*

" He's in a meeting at the moment, is there a message ? "

" It's for that whistleblower series he's doing. I've got some ammo I think he'd… "

" Gosh ! That's *exactly* who he's… " Rose Croft was new on the desk and her grasp of confidentiality still infirm.

" Oh, that's perfect. " *Nothing ventured, nothing gained.* " Probably got Dr. Carlyle in, right ? I was supposed to hook up with him… "

Rose thought it a chance to feed that lovely Charles a plum. " Well, perhaps…why don't I just – what is your name again ? "

" Giacomo Puccini. "

" Oh. You speak *awfully* good… "

But Neale had what he wanted and rang off, quickly exiting the booth to hail a cab.

" Pennington Street, *The Times* offices, and boot it friend. "

Twenty minutes later, Neale defied orders.

" He's at it again Mr. Prinsep. Checked it out. He's been blabbing to Cock...that journalist. Watching him leave the *Times* as we speak – anything special you want done ? "

Bite your tongue, thought Prinsep. He'd always value information over radio silence; there just wasn't enough info, yet. No fresh banner vilifying industry practice, and thus no point cranking up the heat. A minor annoyance, as it left nothing dazzling to impart to his lackey.

That could all change of course, in a flash. Just that morning, two little 'rodents' had scurried onto his desk: a rare hard copy alert from the CEC; followed by an official 'expression of concern', by Qatar if you please.

An aggrieved researcher in Glasgow (Prinsep felt anyone residing in Glasgow *ought* to feel aggrieved) had chosen to warn B.A. of an imminent health sector report. The inevitable bombshell fell from a wholly different quarter of the sky than Carlyle's indictment of false science. Marketing would be tarred as ruthless and cavalier; a load of damning inside documents would paper the media with company mock-ups styled to mimic packs of condoms, a *Smooth-Light* manager's proposed brand slogan – 'the diet Cola of cigarettes' – even a 'lovers' fag, filtered at both ends, to be lit at the middle. The News at 6 would drool over the graphics ! Prinsep cursed the idiots with too much time on their hands and their airy-fairy brainstorming.

Then there was the 'concern'. It registered much like a diplomatic protest, not unbefitting B.A.'s quasi-state relationship with the Gulf. There most certainly would be seismic repercussions if ignored. The veiled allegation was that the tobacco giant was lobbying key Islamic leaders who opposed Quranit anti-smoking measures. The rebuke even attached an undeniable Agenda from Corporate Affairs – *Jesus Christ in the morning !*

" No. Not now Neale…nothing violent, if you can refrain. We need to see what if anything hits the press – by all means track him though. *Haunt* him everywhere. I want to know where the prick is and where he's headed at all times. Am I clear ? "

He put the phone down and turned like a condemned man to the last of the day's clippings:

> ***BBC journalists issued guidelines for health reporting***
>
> *Following criticism from the King's Fund, Health, that Britain's major killers – smoking, alcohol abuse, obesityand mental illness – are statistically under-reported, the Guardian reports that the BBC has set new, aggressive guidelines for its reporters.*

Prinsep thought of the Chairman. Couldn't the sods have put 'obesity' first ? He had a morose vision of 2001 arriving like a barge-load of shit.

**

Sherwood in the twilight, is Robin Hood awake
...Rake away the red leaves, rake away the mould

Alfred Noyes

There isn't a train I wouldn't take
...no matter where it's going

Edna St Vincent Millay

" Welcome to St. Paul's ! Since the year 604, millions have walked up the hill to see the chapel which became one of the world's architectural triumphs... "

The Dean of the Cathedral waxed proud in his regular noon-hour greeting, and faithful servant that he was, injected a gentle admonition.

" Whilst you enjoy the splendour here, which tells the tale of a great nation, do remember St. Paul's is first and foremost a great *church*, a house of God. "

Fair enough, smiled Marie. Though the most sacred act she'd performed in years was recanting the practice of law. On the odd Saturday evening back in Quebec, when she let grandma Yacinthe prevail, Marie would breeze into the Basilica on Rue St. Jean, unrepentant, to eke out the hour mentally cataloguing religious trappings and their link to Rome: the pervasive chauvinism, the eagle lectern and cleric's robes from the legions, etc. And when she tired of that, she proceeded to analyse the volupt 16th and 17th century canvases with which the church had managed to paper its modesty, visualizing the sins the models likely committed after the sittings. Otherwise, Marie had lapsed to the max.

" Karl ! "

A lone pigeon swooped in the Great West Door and flapped wildly overhead. It veered off as far as the nave, before a glare from the Duke of Wellington, saddled for the fray atop his memorial at the same flight level, managed to repel the avian queue-jumper from whence he entered.

The Iron Duke – how thrilling ! 'Ms Rioux was greeted today with pomp and fanfare...' She was a total convert to the Brits' unaffected bond with history. They were undeniably steeped in the stuff, both trivial and magisterial, and not averse to enjoying it. In Canada, Marie reflected, you had to be hurled bodily from a stranger's car in the middle of nowhere before your head struck an overgrown site marker – assuming they hadn't bulldozed it for a much-needed strip-mall.

Marie left the hero of Waterloo and moved into the central dome area and a galaxy of vaults and arches. Midday sun fell through in stately shafts, gilding the rich wall mosaics and Grinling Gibbons wood carving; dynamic figures and plaques etched with derring-do or Latin lurked in alcoves and side chapels everywhere. The air hung pleasantly cool, bathing the record of monarch and commoner in the musk of time.

" Hello everyone. Welcome … "

Marie's little group shifted towards a table and chair in a niche to the left, where a stooped woman in navy blazer and flannel skirt waited with hands clasped, smiling sweetly.

" My name is Vivien. I'm the last of the St. Paul's Fire Watch that was formed in 1939 to patrol the roof for sparks or fire during the Blitz. Now I'm a 'Working Friend', and it's my privilege to answer any questions you may have about the Cathedral… "

But it was another voice, or rather, voices, which floated high above the elderly guardian and drew Marie across the vast floor beneath the dome.

" *Without thy grace we waste away, like flowers that wither and decay…* "

In the ornate stalls of the elevated Quire, two banks of choristers rehearsed for Advent, their antiphony trilling with the purity that thrives on innocence. It was the phrase, '*like flowers…*' which summoned Marie, and, so it seemed, Lilian Nichols; for the ambulance driver stood momentarily at the High Altar of St. Paul's, gazing down through the singers at Marie, the mystery bouquet cradled like an infant in her arms.

The instant he saw her, Neale halted at the stairwell to the Crypt. The pensive, Parisian-looking woman unnerved him – a minor victory he ceded only to divas and great tenors. She seemed enthralled by the music from the Quire, and he, inexplicably, by her. Out of the blue, or rather, the *void* trailing decades back to Carnaby Street and dinners on the Continent, Neale felt suddenly ambushed, preyed upon by an intimacy which transcended latent urges.

Marie, on the other hand, given the wine and letters of the prior evening, and fully in sync from plowing through records at the Commonwealth War Graves Commission and British Red

Cross all morning, faced *her* apparition with equanimity. In fact, she felt moved to conduct a brief exchange.

Yes, Lil, I made some 'enquiries'... didn't know you were born in Canada – Quebec City ! Served in Corsica before Belgium – a real Odyssey. And oh, ma petite, I held your actual death certificate: 'Cause of death - influenza 11 days, broncho-pneumonia' it said, signed by a Canadian doctor, 'Ellis'; he was kind I hope. So unfair...and your brother – but Lil, you must know him by now, and after all, you did save him. Your trick worked, didn't it ? I couldn't find a thing on Joseph – no 'Hébert' or 'Nichols' in any record here. I wonder what your mom did afterwards...but she must be gone and with you both now, surely, and know the story. I'll keep trying. Lots of time to dig around in Surrey...

" Right then, everyone, let's take a stab at '*Creator of the Starry Height*'... "

The voice of the choirmaster jogged Marie's senses and reminded her of the Whispering Gallery, circling grandly overhead. She winked at the nearest chorister – causing wild notoriety for the rest of his day – and strolled back across the floor to the dome stairway.

She took the 259 steps in easy, athletic fashion, leaving Neale gasping an unavoidably discreet distance behind. Once at the Gallery, however, her knees weakened when she peered over the rail to the floor 99 feet below. On a level with the lush murals and the sparkling glass and tile mosaics, she felt like a tiny figurine on one layer of a huge wedding cake.

The ‘thing to do’ urged the guidebook, was to speak something softly to the wall behind you, intended for a person standing diametrically on the other side of the Gallery. The acoustics would carry the ‘whisper’ clearly around the wall to your listener opposite. Marie was alone but gave it a whirl.

“ Je t’aime, je t’aime… ” she breathed throatily, lips pressed to the cool plaster, then giggled, but listened for a second anyway.

“ Je t’adore aussi ”, came the reply back around the dome.

Startled, Marie swung about in time to see the back of a short-ish, male form disappear into the other stairwell. *Give and you shall be rewarded*, she laughed to herself. She shrugged, and proceeded to bound up the next 120 steps to the Stone Gallery. Neale, though smitten, opted to wait below, extending his temporary abandonment of duty.

Marie descended after fifteen minutes with an appetite, and thus hunger and circumstance fused the current objects in Neale’s dim spotlight.

The B&B lady had said not to miss eating ‘amid the ruins’, in the Refectory. ‘A real bistro dear; they do a shi-shi lunch and a proper tea, *in the shadow* of Wellington and Nelson !’

Neale trailed down into the Crypt after Marie like an awkward boy. At one point along the lower corridor, he clung like a lizard to the side of Wellington’s granite tomb while she paused in front of a wall memorial. The tablet bore a likeness, in relief, of Florence Nightingale. Neale, entirely ignorant of the legendary nurse, thrilled instead to the fleeting juncture when the faces of Marie and Flo locked in perfect profile: both shone with their simple cut of hair and firm look of engagement.

Viewer and pursuer moved on and had reached Nelson's casket, fore and aft respectively, when Neale threw caution to the wind and lurched forward, sucking in his breath to say God-knew-what – then froze. As did Marie, just short of the Refectory entrance.

Neale ducked behind a pillar. Both had reacted to the solitary individual ensconced within at a side table covered in crisp linen. His eyes danced with conjecture. His right elbow rested on the table, and he waved his fork in sudden motions, as if conducting a hidden *divertimento*.

Marie went ahead, making a bead for the lone diner.

Thoby looked up and choked on his salad. Well-trained schoolboy that he was, he shot to his feet, spluttering something inaudible. His mixed reverie shifted to a holding pattern, but acquired a radiant hue with this improbable second chance.

" Well Mr. Carlyle, will we ever meet amongst the living ? "

" Th…'Thoby', *please* – remember, the 'very English' name ? " There was new-found resolve, but his mind, razor-sharp just seconds ago, was now jelly.

" Of course… "

" Please join me…only just started…It's smashing seeing you again. " He had every reason to believe how short life was, and at a bare minimum, had no fear of ever again being too transparent with his emotions. The ludicrous option was to sit elsewhere in the empty room, alone. Marie let Thoby guide her chair in, a cheerful victim of the doctrine of coincidence.

" So much to tell…er, so much has happened – for which I apologize, " he added hastily.

" You must have thought me crackers yesterday at Brookwood, yelling out at that 'Nicholson' stone. It was quite the day, though…all added up last night to a real epiphany – forgive the tritism. First I've had since 'Souse' Miller kicked me out of Classics into Science… "

A waiter materialized and Marie let Thoby gather himself while she ordered butternut squash soup and a mango salad. It was an occasion in any sense, but with the prospect of further revelations, she ordered a large carafe of Chardonnay.

" 'Thoby' it is, and I'm all ears, but I may surprise you on the 'epiphany' thing. Her name was '*Nichols*' by the way, and you won't believe what you stumbled on …but let's hear you first. This *is* the perfect venue for plots and confessions… " The wine arrived. Marie raised her glass and fixed the erstwhile whistleblower with a conspiratorial smile. " Here's to a Surrey cemetery, and life after death ! "

Thoby concentrated on not breaking his glass. There'd been nothing in his world to celebrate for ages and the toast hit him as eerily attuned to his current rebirth.

Neale hovered out of sight, gripped by mild apoplexia. A dark angel had just stung him on the job, proceeded to entice him back to his 'rabbit', and Jesus Christ, then sat down and cozied up for lunch with the jerk ! How could he threaten one and impress the other while they were together ?

But the demands of Neale's retainer paled quickly in his little quandary. It was no prod that his affair with B.A. was on the skids. The firm had developed cold feet over strikes on its own people, and *sub rosa* contracts, Carlyle and his dead pal aside, had dropped sharply – dependable, tidy product notwithstanding. The friggin' train wreck didn't look so lucky now; probably spooked Prinsep. Prinsep, who stepped on Neale at *every* opportunity.

Neale leered from the wings like a Peter Lorre rental, held by the grey-green poise in the young woman's eyes. He blinked when she shed her vest and stretched her arms behind, extending a full chest towards Thoby without inhibition. Neale felt this was the sort of woman other women admired, and he lapsed into fantasy. He imagined guiding her down the aisle at La Scala, and generally leading the champagne life, thanks to the blood money he'd salted in villages around Europe.

Thoby had forgotten his duck terrine.

" You're so congenial. I mean, without even knowing me. And right now I'm so agitated, I even *feel* obnoxious. 'Heady with resolve' as they say in novels… "

" But that's exciting. Off on an adventure ? "

Yes…yes, that's exactly what it must be. It sounded much brighter than 'atonement' .

" Bang on. So here's the 'nutshell' if you can bear it – summon the constabulary if not – why you found me secreted in my own version of Rumpole's wine bar, plotting to 'kick ass' as you Yan…whoops, Canadians would say. " He didn't hesitate to call himself a spade: " I'm nobody of course, but for the moment, I'm notorious throughout Her Majesty's realm. A dreaded 'whistleblower'… " Thoby looked calmly around. " What I have fathomed now about my former masters, together with my status as a traitor, leads me to believe hiding is actually a good thing. But, while not seen, I do urgently need to be *heard* over the next while… "

Was she lunching with an affable paranoid on the lam, Marie wondered.

" I'm not paranoid, in the probable case you're wondering. I have a true history, a *shameful* history, and I have to make amends… I saw myself as child victim I suppose, 'betrayed' by a father who killed himself instead of sticking around; underneath I needed to impress him. But years later, when my thesis on tobacco-specific nitrosamines made the Lancet, I betrayed *myself*, wilfully blinded by luxury clubs, Bentleys, best seats in London theatres, an obscene salary, and all the sugar coating British Andorra Tobacco's hook. For those bloody pirates, it was simply good strategy to have a Cambridge nerd on the masthead. " Even as he rebuked himself, he sped off into the end clip from *Casablanca*, where he assured Marie of the beginning of a beautiful relationship…

Marie felt a genuine impulse, patiently summarizing. " So you launched yourself with a tobacco giant… "

" They pimped on my degree…'Yes, Dr. Carlyle, ours *is* a controversial industry in challenging times, but you can make a positive difference, a legitimate difference. Fully funded, you can explore every avenue towards a safer cigarette – face it, most smokers don't quit, and you're in a position to do a service for them, something an army of health groups could never hope to.' "

Short weeks before, Marie would have killed to act against a tobacco company; as a woman, she had always been incensed by the '*you've come a long way baby*' ads, yet here she felt herself empathizing. So many times she'd heard clients in the agony of true remorse beg to plead 'guilty with an explanation'. In Thoby's instance, Marie already saw a promising mind diverted, a pampered life in shreds, and a belated quest for pardon.

" How's the vino, helps digest my rambling I hope. Shall I press on ? "

" Please, I'm fascinated. " But she did reach for the carafe.

" Never smoked you know. Mom smoked when I was young, veritable prairie on fire, stack from Newcastle. So did everybody it seemed, now I think of it. Guess that made fags less sinister for me…later though, intellectually, I was complicit. No excuse. And I made my mark alright, disgraced my father's name and more. The last few months, I've been a wreck, couldn't stand myself. I'd get up in the morning, stare helplessly at my wife then flee outside – only to crawl back when I ran into school kids at the Green, all zany and full of hope and expectations. I felt like a scythe in a field of flowers… "

A shock of sandy hair fell relentlessly over Thoby's right eye, inducing Marie to look on him more as an eager school-boy than the earnest flagellant.

" You're used to listening aren't you – bloody marvelous, you suffering through my…my 'St. Paul's Epistle to the Canadians'. But your showing up has made things upbeat, dare I say, a *launch* occasion. If I can press on, then it's all yours in a jiffy, but it's *your* memory which figures in this last bit… "

No need to bow and scrape. There was the familiar rush in hearing a new client's tale of woe, except here, what twigged her 'better angels' was the motive: it had real consequence, could touch millions young and old. This was no scummy drug-dealer, or HM the Queen *vs* Me, Me, Me. All this Thoby craved – she could feel it coming – was *a way back.* A warm sensation ran through her as if this lunch had always been scheduled.

" *My* memory…? "

" You quoted Tennyson yesterday and I couldn't get poets out of my mind for hours until some Housman returned, and I remembered the 'land of lost content'. Something about 'happy highways' where one can't go again, and I woke up wondering why *can't* we go back ? Back to those ruddy sign-posts and make better choices ? "

" No doubt in *my* mind Thoby – why not ? Do what you feel you should, and can, no blessing needed… " Her eyes smiled directly into him. Poets tumbled in their haste to pour out of him now; there was Cummings and 'voices in their eyes…'

" It's *High Noon* and it's time for me to get out of Dodge… " He wrestled with his favourite metaphor. " The evil in my career is stark. It begs smiting. It's become an honest-to-God, Scrooge-gets-a-life reversal for me – *dreams* Marie ! I think

I've cheated myself and not allowed dreams to take hold: I need to bury regret with *real* dreams. "

She hated to put a pin in his enthusiasm, or his oxymoron, but was curious. " And what of your wife in all this, you mentioned...? "

" Dead. Riddled with cancer at 39...smoker of course, fellow exec at B.A. Tireless user of the product that paid her. She was the marketing guru with our French sub, *Brun-Guillaume et Fils*. Spent all her time in Paris, Barcelona and Andorra. She was part of the squad that head-hunted me. Started coughing blood a week after my first internal squawk about suppressed science... "

Thus far, Neale had picked up on 'Brookwood', 'Marie', 'yesterday', and another 'cemetery'. But he wasn't taking notes, just staring at Marie.

" At first there was silence, and what I'd carved for myself gradually came into focus, ie. no *valuable* life, no control. Meanwhile, my wife went straight downhill. I leaked some findings, and the D.T.I. announced an inquiry. B.A. cancelled our special health insurance not long after, just as Sarah was carted off to the Sloan-Kettering in New York. "

Such corporate malice, relayed first-hand, stunned Marie.

" I think, on balance, she never got it, even when things unraveled...or maybe she did, but refused to admit she'd killed herself in a wretched cause. The last morning, I found her sitting at her computer in the den, her fingers unable to turn the pages in a stack of new data from East Asia. She was hacking and gurgling, then suddenly went still and whispered something utterly uncharacteristic: ‘sandalwood, sweet white… quinquireme’, and she gazed out the window.

‘Never roamed did we…babies, rowing stately home…’ ”

Marie felt not the least awkward, only saddened. “ Oh, I can’t… ”

Thoby saw the moisture forming in her eyes and hurried on. “ We had no children you see – no time in her agenda – never traveled anywhere memorable together. When she died in her chair, I lost a business associate, not a soul-mate. ”

Marie, ever the counselor and resilient ear, felt compassion. She looked through the clutter of glasses between them and saw a would-be crusader at his last supper, and couldn’t help caring. In the same reflection, her own past crept forward. It struck her as the perfect moment to ‘out’ it, thereby distracting Thoby.

“ Don’t think you’re alone; there are great holes in my childhood too…and as for ‘career’, I try not to think of the sewer-rats I’ve helped release. Some recrimination or disappointment is healthy – it led me here, where I met you, and together we found Lilian, didn’t we ! No, anguish isn’t all wasted, it can produce the highest good – so go for it ! ” She had a bit of a flow going.

“ Funny, the parallels. *My* father took off when I was a baby. I wouldn’t know him if he fell in front of me. My mother sealed the coffin on all connections, except to refer to him as a ‘slime bucket’. So in my case, it was *myself* I chose to impress – strange isn’t it, neither of us mentioned *mothers* in the equation

– thought I'd win the little guy's wars, be everybody's hero. Move on to conquer the world without becoming a B.B. … "

" 'B.B.' ? "

" *Banshee Bimbo*: annoying sub species – you know, that whines if she's not senior partner next week, blames men *always*, and dresses to convert eunuchs…but I eventually fell off my high horse. I got down on my 'calling' to the point where I saw it merely as a trade. Too many egos living vicariously in the sordid trenches. Weeks went by without an intelligent conversation, just conniving, slick talk, nothing but gamesmanship and nobody really 'winning', form without substance – the shallow metaphors go on – and I began to see my finer senses orphaned. And then of course, I couldn't tolerate a mediocre marriage, and a man who could. *My* ex didn't die, but he might as well have… "

Apart from acting on the intuition that spirited her from Quebec, Marie hadn't paused for self-analysis since leaving – except for a rough night on the freighter, and the fleeting nightmare which suggested the true compulsion behind her exit was 'finding' her father. What energized her at the moment was pursuing the Brookwood experience, putting flesh on the larger context, family or otherwise.

" So let me fill you in on Ms Nichols ! Your past is unquestionably driving you Thoby, now so is mine, it turns out. Only I didn't see it coming. My roots are shadowy, especially the 'anglo' side, but when you called me over to that stone, " and she smiled wryly at sounding like a cheap psychic, " it must have been a sign… "

Thoby flushed. Something in common ! He sat on his elation.

" No. You don't say ? "

" You and I both read the inscription yesterday, and it was moving, but that was that and we left – then get this. Last night at dinner, I opened a bundle of correspondence from the First War era which my mom had stuffed in my bag. She'd apparently never read it herself, but knew enough about it to say it might liven up my travels – and who do you suppose threads her way through the letters: *Lilian Beatrice Nichols* ! We're *related* ! It's almost as if she tapped you on the shoulder when she felt me nearby. I tell you Thoby, she's going to haunt me (she didn't yet care to throw in her 'sighting' at the High Altar a half hour earlier, and the inner bells that rang in response). I spent all morning searching her life and death, but she's pleading that more be done. I can *feel* it. "

Neale had progressed from fidgeting to grinding his teeth. He could easily have whacked Carlyle twice already that morning, except for his new orders. It was too much that he now had to watch the creature who'd jolted his libido nuzzle the target. And there was another aspect to the scenario he couldn't fathom: something about the female kept tripping muffled alarms, which only set him more on edge. That edge instantly manufactured an obsessive moral rage. It galled that this freaking whistleblower, by rights a traitor in anyone's book, should be all smiles and sucking back the bubbly, instead of cowering in Neale's presence. He ought to have been begging for a deal, and while he was at it, surrendering the woman to the better man.

The aroma of coffee and *crème brulé* passing sent Neale off once again on his European tour. He saw the Crypt brighten, whirl from its bearings, and fill with the rising strains of *The Blue Danube*. Thoby disappeared, and Neale replaced him around Marie. Sam and the Hapsburgs, waltzing on…

" Just to let you know, we close in twenty minutes ", advised the waiter gently, anxious not to lose his sole gratuity of the afternoon.

" Two brandies then, to seal the future… " volunteered Marie. " When our paths cross again, I'll tell you what my investigations – all your fault – have revealed. And of course, you will be assuring me that an evil empire is reeling from your blows ! "

" That's all quite astonishing, truly…*mindboggling*, the coincidence. " Was his own upheaval causing sympathetic revelations in others ? He didn't want to let her go. " But that *chance* discovery means you didn't come all this way just to rattle the family closet; was there not a wish list of places or things ? "

" I'd like to see *real* 'tinkers' somewhere on a road, like to sit in the late afternoon in the Tuileries watching the human parade – after a day in the Louvre of course, hmm…hang out in an old 'spy' hotel, Swiss probably, see the Eiger at sunrise, do a long run through the Loire valley – so yes, lots, but no set itinerary. Except…oh ! For sure, a pilgrimage to the Isle of Wight and *Dimbola*, Julia Cameron's home – she was the guiding star in my Victorian studies – every male should have to go there too. I imagine standing with her at the back gate, waiting for Tennyson to drop in, then looking the other way, down Terrace Lane, for the local kids and great figures to come strolling innocently by, only to fall prey to her camera. I'm forever starting out on that lane you know – it's a mantra image, a frozen moment in time – like that May dancing scene that opens Polanski's *Tess.* "

The brandy arrived. *This is it*, thought Thoby.

" Marie, " as they clinked snifters, " here's the scheme. I've chucked everything. Got papers and cash in Switzerland I mean to liberate in the time left to me, which may be in short supply – who knows – I just want to get out there, do battle and move on. "

Was that *his* voice ? *Here goes…*

" I've a ticket on tonight's *Eurostar*, used my credit card, but won't be taking it. Instead, I'm heading over to Victoria Station to grab ye old channel packet for France – pay cash of course… " He took a swig for more bravado. " And I wonder, would… would you take a second ticket – my tab of course, not to insult you or assume anything – but go with me ! See what comes down the proverbial, re-chart our courses. Sounds like you're already well under-way, and…well, you do have 'adventurer' written all over (he was dying to say 'your gorgeous face'). No strings of course, raise the walls of Jericho whenever…soak up every vista you mentioned, and some weird *boîtes* to boot, and… and your criminal wisdom can guide my avenging stealth. "

Thoby's face blanched, his zeal momentarily drained with the Herculean effort of laying his shy self naked on the cutting board.

" Shocked you haven't I. Ruined everything, what ? " He felt like one of the suitors in a P.G.Wodehouse tale. But as romance and blind gusto won through for those hapless heroes, so giddy resolve kept Thoby buoyant.

As Thoby spoke, the waiter reappeared, admonished by a £10 note from Neale and the juicy info that the pair he served were in fact lesser royalty on a shameful tryst, to deposit a silver tray.

" Good God ! "

" What – *Thoby !* I pay my own shot… "

" No, no dear lady. Look ! " And he slid over a glossy photo from under the bill. It showed the two of them in earnest confab, taken, obviously, just minutes before.

" That's an odd sort of promotion… " began Marie.

" Waiter ! " The server hadn't quite made it behind the Chinese screen. " Who gave this to you ? "

" To be honest sir, I was unaware of this being on the tray. I do apologize if there has been some intrusion, but I've no idea where this came from… " After a moment of awkward mutual reflection, the waiter beat a hasty second retreat.

Thoby leapt up and raced to the entrance, looked wildly around, then steamed back, waving his arms and muttering into space. " How stupid ! So melodramatic… " Perturbed as he was, in resuming his seat, the simple beauty of his companion calmed him. " No promotion Marie, a *warning*. A calling card; B.A. wants me to know they're keeping tabs – *Bollocks !* I've put you at risk… " And then, in a shamelessly crass pleading, " Even more reason to leave for a while, d'you think ? "

Despite this minor upheaval, instinct flirted with the idea of actually going. Marie let a large splash of brandy burn down her throat and pushed her chair back from the table, resting both hands on her lap and scrutinizing Thoby – *he* thought, in a withering fashion – as if debating whether to cross-examine. *The 'old channel packet' !* Would 'the fat man' lurch around the deck in a fierce gale to snare them in a bizarre web ?

As often happens following a glimpse of the inevitable, the mind concocts a supporting rationale. Marie now had what seemed a prescient flash from her morning coffee. A half-page etching in the Travel section of the *Guardian* had made a deep impression, perhaps because she was relaxed and her defenses down. It spurred her crusade to restore the unknown to contemporary life; it depicted, against a sweeping background, the intrepid Sir Richard Burton, planted on the prow of a dug-out, somewhere in pursuit of the Nile's elusive origin. She'd yielded outright as a conscript to his eccentric, virile command, floating dreamy and disquieted for fully half an hour in Marita's deep leather chair.

" There's only one thing to do in a situation like this. "

She'd left the poor man hanging. " What's that? "

" Haven't a clue to be honest, but doesn't the hero always says that at this point … "

His good-natured segue surprised her. Not quite as rakish as Sir Richard, but very…*boyish*, in a lovable way. In search of better goals, yet someone who'd already discovered the source of his river of discontent. Marie teased him.

" Certain conditions would apply Thoby. Croissants for instance, daily, with loads of jam, black currant preferably. Café au lait, and Sunday papers from the world's capitals. *Walking* wherever possible. And unquestioning tolerance should I slip totally into the 19th century here and there… "

Thoby felt cruel in realizing how Sarah held an extinguished candle to this sympathetic creature – where *had* she hidden all his wasted indenture ? What a beacon she might have been. " I'd expect nothing less from a lawyer. Where do I sign ? "

For the moment, Marie remained the professional, skilled at disengagement. And of course, she was attractive, a mixed blessing which demanded frequent exercise of such art.

" I'm touched – no, that's condescending – I'm *honoured* by your invitation Thoby. It's sincere, and I know it will be an adventure to wind back to those 'happy highways'. Meeting Lilian makes me think I should check my own map… " She looked him square in the eyes. " I know the time and place; if it all fits, I may show. Fair enough ? " Marie stood brusquely, leaned over and pressed her hand around Thoby's forearm.

More than a handshake, less than a hug. What did he expect, or deserve ? His heart sank, though it had been a glorious interlude. Still seated because he read her desire to leave without fuss, and more because he didn't wish to be left standing like a fool a second time, Thoby cast one final lure.

"You've been the champagne to christen my expedition. I only hope to see you later… " He jammed the photo into a pocket as a keepsake, rather than the crude threat he knew it was. She reached the archway. " Just in case, by 'later', the idea is to be snug in the *Schweizerhof* in Bern by tomorrow evening. Could have Mr. LeCarré greet you… "

Marie half-turned and waved. As if changing gear, she flicked her auburn hair and headed off, forcing Neale behind a cloth divider to the pantry. Her scent brushed his pocked face. Amazingly, it was familiar – *Bluebell* – because someone once had begged him to buy the very same.

Marie didn't look back for any further reaction to her exit. She had a clear last image: the expectant schoolboy seated under a huge print of Whistler's *Nocturne*, waiting perhaps to 'go up' to Cambridge, the world before him. Tousled hair, worn hacking jacket, jeans, and collarless blue shirt that matched his eyes, which were shining with emotion. Gentle hands were locked in front of him on the table. Resolute certainly, but very much alone in a 'thin place'.

She got as far as the boutique on the opposite side of the lower hall. A poster in the display window charmed her and she bought it. It was a 1917 Edmund Dulac graphic entitled '*The Sisters*'. A 'land girl', a nurse, and a munitions worker clasped hands. Marie thought they looked so bright and committed in their roles, paying a subordinate's price, but playing. The unrequited antidote to man's persistent folly.

On the way out, Marie made a point of speaking to 'Vivien'. She found her still at her post, sipping milky tea.

" Hello again. I meant to ask you about life during the Blitz and your dangerous work – if you don't mind. "

" Oh my no, it's kind of you to ask – not many do. It was such an intense time you know, for a young woman, for everyone. I remember not sleeping properly for months… "

" What stands out most of all in your memory ? "

The pale skin tautened over what clearly had been a striking face, her eyes glistened and grew almost fierce; age retreated. She reminded Marie of a benign Virginia Woolf.

" Well, there *was* one night in particular – I can't remember the exact date, but sometime just after Christmas, 1940 – and hell was in the air. There's no other way to describe it dear… "

As she spoke, Vivien stared up into the dome.

" There were 40 of us on a shift usually, and I was paired with Tommy Prendergast. We were patrolling the narrow balcony which circles the dome outside – see, there dear – the Stone Gallery, 74 feet above the Whispering Gallery. Things were terrifying: smoke, flames, the long low whistle of falling bombs – they told us there were 1500 fires in London from that one raid – sirens everywhere, things dusted with snow and very cold. So many nooks and crannies up there, and pockets of black where you couldn't see your way. You were always afraid of stepping off into the sky where some railing had been blown away…then there was a hit nearby which shook the whole roof and some masonry fell directly on poor Tommy – knocked him flat. "

Marie fully expected Noel Coward, Vera Lynn, and a troop of smoke-smeared Wardens to appear; she was spellbound by the recollections of this frail, spirited woman.

" Immediately I turned to see him go down, there was a roar like a freight train entering the station, then a monstrous crash and thud right behind me – the impact lifted me off my feet and threw me half over the railing. But instead of screaming, I remember a wild energy jolted me. I picked myself up and got on with my task, which seemed simple. I scrambled towards the 'thud', and as an arc lamp swung round I was able to see the tail of a huge incendiary – unexploded of course, or I wouldn't be here telling you this dear – swaying side to side over the walkway at eye-level. I peeked down towards its nose and there seemed clear space all around its body – I had no idea what was supporting it. It looked to me like it might slip through the dome wall at any moment and go off on the floor far below, just a few feet from where we are now… "

A shiver ran dutifully through Marie. The detail was so vivid. " Please, have some more of your tea before it gets cold. "

" I tore the rope we carried from Tommy's belt and crouched under the tail end of the bomb. I made several loops in the mid portion of the line and slid them over the tail and pulled them tight, if you can imagine… " Marie tried. " then I tied both ends to the rail several feet apart, hoping it would hold the thing for a while. "

Marie almost forgot she herself had left a man in 'danger' below. " What happened then, Vivien – you don't mind me…? "

" Not at all dear. Well, I dragged Tommy to the stairs, if that's what you mean, and carried him all the way down, and then… I dragged him to the *altar* ! " She smiled cheerfully. " I was Mrs. Prendergast for fifty happy years, but you know – what is your name then love ? "

" Marie… "

" Marie, it was so exhilarating, that one moment, I was so *alive* then…never felt quite that way again. I'm so pleased I did the right thing and faced the challenge…oh dear, I must be boring you with all this memory stuff. "

" Not in a million years dear lady – what extraordinary times you lived through ! And the bomb ? "

" Oh, they managed to get it off the roof without exploding, and everyone made quite a fuss; they gave me the *George Cross* afterwards. I guess I just belong here… "

Marie gave her a kiss on the cheek, shook her hand and thanked her, promising to drop by next time she was in London.

Exiting into a deceptively temperate late afternoon, Marie felt she had just left a dramatic film loaded with history. Nazi missiles freefalling amongst the collective spirits of poet, prince, and politician, the Duke protecting Vivien, and…Thoby. Tthe man had wormed his way into the picture.

The past two days – Brookwood, the *Cross Keys*, St. Paul's– lapped at her feet like a prelude to something uniquely beautiful. She possessed the 'wild' energy Vivien had encountered, she just had to identify the 'task'.

Marie stopped under the trees on the south side of the Cathedral. She looked up at the dome she'd seen in books, wreathed in smoke and destruction, and thought of the souls within its sanctuary. Like a cheerful novitiate, she surrendered to all these who'd seized their day, or, on occasion, been seized by it.

One of the pleasures of reading old letters
is the knowledge that they need no answer

Lord Byron

Marie left the tube at Sloane Square, agitated by Thoby's impulsive offer. It required immediate action, affirmative or not; she was incapable of dismissing it out of hand. She couldn't simply go off to dinner and a play and never think of it, or him, again.

The street offered distraction, so she ignored the **#11** double-decker and set out along King's Road, entertaining herself with the chic windows and the occasional Chelsea Pensioner pecking through the upscale hurly-burly. She let her pace shake out the merits of joining Thoby's redemption tour.

For starters, there was empathy with the underdog, salted here with the prospect of lobbing snowballs at a societal mega-demon. Deeper than expert empathy, however, subtle indicators kept prodding that it was a 'gut' thing; and in addressing instinct, Marie, incurably fair, had to admit Carlyle was lovable, in a goofy, holes-in-the-elbow, Harris Tweed way. His brain showed vital signs, yet he came across as self-deprecating and unaffectedly boyish. There was a tangible attraction, so, *why the hell not ?*

Well, she countered, attempting prudence, was it a winner move to 'enlist' at the whim of a guilt-racked male, one who lacked the status of even a one-night stand, and who'd screwed up his life – at least in his own, male-martyr terms ?

There was nothing restricting her to London of course, except merry old England itself, which, as they said, there'd always be; so perhaps the issue didn't beg romantic evaluation, and was more, 'will Rioux take the case' and help spank the bad guys.

But none of her ruminations mattered ultimately, with Lilian hovering. Her continued presence hinted at a more compelling motive. The jilted nuns back at Quebec must have been working voodoo, as in the past 24 hours, Marie had fallen into an intense eddy of fact and emotion. A slab in a country graveyard, heartfelt letters from the roar and aftermath of history, linked by a girl *of her own flesh and blood*, who shadowed Marie right into St. Paul's ! Throw in the engaging whistleblower, with whom she now stood framed, literally – on a silver tray no less – and Marie could almost look back and see Vivien, her slight form cradled by the Cathedral pillars, shooing her on to meet the challenge, the task…

She drew even with Chelsea's Old Town Hall in no time at all and walked left down Oakley, into the exotic catacombs of rock-star, magnate, bourgeois, and glitterati – ghosts and incarnations. As she passed the flower-boxed Georgian windows, the skylights and anomalous balconies, she speculated what wines were being served on those mahogany tables that evening, what corporate assassinations schemed, what islet off Majorca annexed – other people's lives, and that brought her back to Thoby.

But a clump of perfumed foliage – November notwithstanding – feathered Marie's hair to announce she'd rounded 'Upper' Cheyne onto Cheyne Row, and her room, *her* room ! She could hardly believe she showered looking over a rear garden to a stone wall which hid mulberry trees planted by Elizabeth I in Henry VIII's backyard.

Flashing blue lights quickly re-set her focus.

An ambulance and squad car blocked the narrow street in front of Number 30. Marita was standing on the step talking excitedly to a male and female officer. Seeing Marie, she threw up her arms and rushed forward.

" Marita ! "

" It's terrible ! There's been a burglary Marie, minutes ago… one got away in a car, but I got the other one with Hendrik's cricket ball…I'm so very sorry. " Whereupon, the ambulance sped off.

It was fleeting, but Marie noticed as the siren started up that it appeared to scare off an individual coming up Cheyne from the Embankment. In that flicker, she entertained and rejected the notion it was the same male as the whisperer in St. Paul's; though this time, she recorded a swarthy face and mustache.

With much experience on the dark side of the street, Marie's initial reaction was measured. In fact, she thought it droll she should have to go overseas to suffer crime firsthand. She did however, pat her belt reflexively: passport, cash, and cards were all there.

" Not to worry Marita, please, just glad *you're* okay... "

" Perhaps your lodger would go up now with the Constable ma'am. Check what's missing from her room... "

Marie complied, and the two women proceeded to the third floor.

" Yours seems the only room touched, Miss. We can't say why...maybe they were interrupted by Mrs. Clarke – would *you* have any reason to suspect you were targeted ? "

" Absolutely none, " said Marie. *Until this afternoon.* On brief reflection that still seemed too bizarre, and yet, they *had* been sighted together twice in the last two days...

Her mother's folder was gone, and all its contents. As was her lap-top; force of habit had brought it with her so it wouldn't be a tragic loss, but the letters...Marie swayed for an instant as tears flooded her vision. As much as her recorded heritage had grown even sparser, she felt she'd somehow betrayed Lilian.

Marie composed herself.

" If a leather folder, antique-looking, with an 'R' stamped on it and old correspondence inside, turns up, here's my name and... " And at that moment, she decided to go. " Well anyway, I won't know exactly where I'll be in the next while, but I'll check in from time to time... "

" That's fine Miss. Sorry about whatever's missing. I must tell you that in these cases, whatever they can't sell they just dump somewhere, and it's not likely to turn up again…it must be specially upsetting when you're away from home. "

Right here looked good for my new home – ah well, the lightness of being a tramp abroad…all she had to do was pack a few things and park the big suitcase with the obliging Marita, then shove off once more, to return anytime…

**

Outside St. Paul's, a young couple trundled a stroller through the fringes of rush hour. Their small male passenger was intent on dogs, squirrels, motor cycles, sea-gulls, the constant helicopter above the Parliament – the whole wide world. A breeze caught his fair hair and streamed it in long wisps over his eyes. For several minutes, Thoby found himself mimicking the boy's head as he rolled it round and round, eyes closed, nosing the fresh air. Except the child's hair looked so much finer.

Thoby headed left down a narrow lane that trickled towards the Thames and a familiar tea-room. Along the way, he ripped up his Eurostar ticket and tossed it in a bin. He also stopped at a booth where he left a voice message for Somers-Cocks to the effect that, in a few days, he would receive some 'hot docs' via secure fax, phone alert to precede sending of same. Then he ducked into *The Barque and Bite* tea-room and ordered a fullsome tea, as he did poorly with food on the Channel. When the scones arrived, he looked up suddenly at the waitress.

" Do you by any chance have some *blackcurrant* jam ? "

**

Marie left the taxi at Victoria Station at 6:30 p.m., about the same hour she'd wandered into the *Cross Keys* the evening before. Time and tide had accelerated since, but she felt quite rational buying a one-way to Paris, via Newhaven, Dieppe and Rouen.

She 'sailed', not from compulsion, nor any immediate fear, though it was mildly unnerving that anyone should abuse a stranger merely because they strayed into this Thoby's path.

**

Thoby, in a supreme effort aided by single malt (father's flask) and sheaves of paper plotting the next drop for the *Times*, clawed his way pretty well back down to earth. A woman in her early 40's, very short camel-hair skirt and cream turtleneck, sashayed by his window. How in God's name could he expect a bright beauty to drop everything and throw in with his feeble purge ? A grey curtain of reality crashed down on Thoby's little panto. He didn't even bother keeping a look-out.

As a consequence, at 7:47 p.m. sharp, Marie and Thoby rattled down to the coast in a soft drizzle, *Second Class,* unaware they occupied adjacent compartments.

Part IV

A Tramp Abroad

(12)

At Newhaven, Thoby bolted through the queue of tourist coaches and lorries for Customs and the ferry, thinking to limit exposure.

Marie, thoroughly bemused with her decision – departing on ‘the uncertain wave’ – sauntered through the Transmanche terminus. She felt the seed of affection, or she wouldn’t be there, but no immediate pressure to hook up with her whistleblower. Instead, she took time to inhale the chill night air with its salt tang, and to listen to the ocean licking outside the departure shed – there was something so helpless yet reassuring about the scrub-board grate of beach stones.

Marie boarded, climbed to the stern deck, and slid onto a life-vest storage compartment. A warm funnel offered a cozy back-prop, and from there, she marked the receding shore. Though with none of the *tristesse* in uprooting from Quebec; more a bracing dash of intrigue.

No ‘fat man’ appeared in due course, but it was impossible in that setting for any school- child not to think of Masefield’s ‘*Dirty British coaster with a salt-caked smokestack, Butting through the Channel...*’ The line repeated itself in sync with the thumping of the *Dieppe*'s engines until Marie at length drew something personal from the poet's lament for the golden times. After numerous bottles of *Mort Subite* on a distant soirée, a young exchange prof from Grenoble had pumped her on how she'd re-order life if faced with the imminent end of the world. More intrigued at the time with how he'd be in bed, Marie had replied glibly she would feel more justified in pursuing her existing affaire with Victorian luminaries.

And therein, a message: her wandering was legit – not that she gave a damn for anyone's approval – but now she understood its value beyond the precious tracking of a more lyrical age. Her leaving Canada and a 'career', her communing with Lilian and Thoby, combined to blow off any taint of whimsy. As she mulled this over, partly to placate imagined protestations from her Mom, Marie noted she *was* crossing to Dieppe on a 'mission', over water which had claimed her grandfather: people, alive and dead, worth caring for.

She remained comfortable playing her own game, one which rejoiced in peculiar behaviour if so desired. Her vagabonding was far from dissipation, firmly in step with being.

Marie felt herself edging closer to a life of one's own...

**

Prinsep was his usual font of congeniality.

" What do you mean, 'he's gone' ? "

" Gone, " repeated Neale flatly, " saw him get a ticket at Waterloo this morning – used his AmEx… "

" How could you lose him ? "

" Didn't lose him. He never showed for the train. "

" You lost him… "

Fuck you, Prinsep. " I'm still certain he's headed for Geneva – my old territory, you remember. I can easily nail… "

" Hands off, *even if* you find him, Neale. Just find out what the hell he's cooking up. " Though Prinsep wouldn't have minded at all if Carlyle suffered an alpine tragedy. " He squawked to the paper again this morning. We'll wait on what crawls out of that, if anything. If something sudden happens just after a media bomb, it won't look good, so…what's this about a woman? "

Neale regretted mentioning her, but then, if he made her seem sinister, they'd want him to keep closer. His delusion blossomed.

" They seemed pretty intimate. Possible recent meeting somewhere else…talked about documents, a cemetery, even a name which I forget for the moment – I'd have to really follow up. "

" You *do* that Neale, and don't lose the bugger again. If she's not media then I want to know what… " His rodent instinct already sounded the alarm about this whole dynamic. He also began to think Neale was losing corporate benefit in these precarious times. The blunt instrument was no longer an attractive M.O.

Neale hit the first digits for Switzerland on his mobile before Prinsep quit the land line at Waterloo. A strategy of sorts formed. It meant hanging briefly in England, so he planted messages on the continent with several officials in his repertoire, it now being evening: the operations chief, Geneva International Airport; the chief manager, Swiss Federal Railways; the Director General of the Schweizer Zoll; and last, the director of the Banque de Lausanne, where B.A. execs often nipped in to squirrel their lucre. Any arrival, comings and goings, by the likely party or parties in question, Neale wanted to know. If exiting, they were to be closely examined, especially for company documents, but no rough handling of the woman, if present.

Next, our man in Fleet scarfed a cheeseburger from an ubiquitous franchise, then left the station for a bleak pub near Blackfriars Bridge. There he made a slobbering fool of himself by consuming an entire bottle of *Veuve Clicquot*, convinced that if only she would turn up in Geneva, he'd easily forgive her poor judgment and they would be ideally launched on a grand tour. And Carlyle, well, he'd be launched into another world altogether, if Neale could sell it to Prinsep. Or even if he couldn't...

By the fifth glass, Neale heard Prinsep snarling, 'You *do* that Neale…' It jacked up his resolve to rifle every scrap of data on the couple – no harm in digging some English dirt while he waited confirmation on any movements across the channel.

Purely from a desire to enhance his working environment, Neale's publican host eventually dumped him into a taxi. On the way home, Neale tried feebly to recall the few words he'd filed away from the Crypt that afternoon. Within an hour of throwing up in his Belgravia flat, Neale felt caged and was back at Waterloo, this time en route to a dingy B&B in Woking. There he would be well-positioned to pursue the next day's enquiries.

**

Thoby spent the best part of the voyage in the forward salon. He sank into a huge chair, having thought it best not to look back, in every sense. The whirlwind of plotting expiation, his mercurial lunch at St. Paul's and the brutal subsequent awakening – and the scotch – quickly put him in a doze.

He couldn't say whether it was an angel or a nurse, but a sheltering presence soon whispered that he'd faltered, *yes indeed*, but it would be 'better', he was on a fine course. Directly, he felt the lead fall from his shoulders, the wounds heal, and himself free to step into the future – a place he'd all but recently abandoned. Then he slept, between the shores.

He woke in the pre-dawn on the French side to the cacophony of horns and general disembarking, with a fantastically clear dream image in his mind. It featured a man standing on a bridge over the Danube, very early in the morning, buoyant with the joy of existence on any terms, refusing to look behind, over the one side – where the flow was brown and turgid and the 21st century seeped in – instead gazing so intently, it was like breathing through his eyes, at the azure streams and indigo eddies of the 19th century, sparkling and dancing away out the other side, and fixing on preserving those pools in his heart: the twilight of imperial culture, the style, grace, artifice and romance of history. And whenever he cared to, or needed to, he could come to that bridge, that side of the bridge, and always be inspired by the vision he'd saved…

Marie and Thoby finally fell in with each other on the mini-bus which bounced them from the port, now estranged almost 15 minutes from the old *centre de ville*, to the train station, a classic great barn. At around 5:00 a.m., a two-car diesel tore out of the continuing drizzle for Rouen.

" I can't believe it, tremendous luck ! How wonderful this – I don't deserve… "

Perhaps not, but I'm game. " We'll let circumstance judge ", Marie smiled sweetly, but she had a warm sensation in all the right places. " I've never been on the lam before… "

**

Paris, Gare St.-Lazare

" This is *so* bad ! " Marie gloated, sipping her glass of Beaujolais. A croissant and café au lait sat waiting at her elbow. She glanced round the elderly station in a pleasant drowse. Even the house plonk had cachet in such a venue. Splinters of grey morning light suspended a century of emotional dust, but even they held promise.

Of the creatures propped against the brass rail and white marble bar at 7:50 a.m., Marie and Thoby were arguably the least suspicious. Midnight-navy suits, ties askew, prominent noses, blasé regard, cigarettes of course – even the dogs smoke in France – turtlenecks and leather and day-old whiskers, like a group audition for *A Man and a Woman*. Breakfast in Paris ! If there was any disappointment for Marie, it was that neither Philippe Noiret nor Yves Montand made an entrance.

Thoby craved fresh juice and porridge, but didn't bat a lash in following suit with his companion – how could someone appear so *luminous* after a grotty train and ferry hike ! He looked at Marie and flashed what he adjudged was his best possible gung-ho smile.

" On to the frontier and Schweiz ! " he decreed, drowning a brioche in his bowl. " Don't you love that word, 'frontier', sounds so dramatic. The Swiss stood in the aisles and cheered when Steve McQueen rammed his motorcycle into the barbed wire at the 'Swiss frontier' sign. "

" Oh Thoby, you know that never happened in the *real* Great Escape…in fact, there were no Americans involved. "

" Ah yes, but it's the Swiss spirit don't you see, their national pride… "

" They'd have refused him entry, mid-air, " teased Marie. It was encouraging to see him high about something. And he did press on.

" Well, here's some Swiss wisdom for you. Remember the great desert battle of El Alamein ? There's a memorial near Alexandria, and in the guest book, a fellow from Geneva wrote, '*S'il y avait un Suisse comme Dieu, tout cela n'aurait pas passé.*' They're big on their historic neutrality… "

" Neutral with a vengeance, verging on anti-semitic. " Thoby saw he was dealing with an informed person. " Their alpine corps turned back, ie. *doomed*, many a refugee. And aren't they under the gun right now for stashing piles of Nazi loot...? " Marie scanned his eyes; Thoby didn't seem rebuked or peeved, just out of touch perhaps with challenging conversation. They could work on that.

In fact, the 'loot' bit didn't rankle Thoby, as he harboured good intentions for much of his sock of dubloons. And he was genuinely tickled by this dynamic sylph who took no prisoners – like Sarah, but with grace and humour, and no second-hand smoke. " You like to be on top of things don't you ? "

" My favourite position... " Marie kept a straight face behind her coffee; for the moment, she wasn't subject to anyone's sense of propriety.

" We'll give them a run today shall we, my dear 'new partner'. Nix on Geneva by the way, it's off to Bern – remember my mentioning the *Schweizerhof* ? Not a skilled cloak and dagger ploy, I suspect, but throw them off a while. Probably the only smart thing I did in the last twenty years...key papers and money in Bern, don't know what inspired me at the time... anyway, Geneva's far too bland for you Marie. "

" So, how... "

" Train to Besançon, bus over the ridge to La Chaux de Fonds, above Neuchâtel, then train to Bern. Quite lovely really... " He was keen to sound more organized and harnessed. " There's a Roman ruin on the far side of Lake Neuchâtel, and a Suchard chocolate factory on the edge of town: everything the inquiring mind and stomach could crave ! Though, alas, you may run into more of that local false bravado. The good burghers of La Chaux de Fonds still brag about the Allied bombs dropped on them by mistake one night instead of France. "

" Just bribe me with an authentic fondue before your nice colleagues pick us off… " Marie quipped, surprised at how cavalier one could foolishly be. " By the way, I should tell you what happened at my B&B yesterday after our lunch… "

" Marie… " For the first time, Thoby felt an intimacy in just speaking her name. " I truly don't know what to say. You've met a total stranger, listened patiently to his wretched travails, and, thrown in with him – wher*ever* did you come from ! "

" No big deal. I suspect we mesh somehow Thoby, and your venture is a worthy option. " She spoke in a wonderfully soft yet firm tone.

" What I mean is, I want to thank you, don't know how to thank you…I've failed my father and my science, failed as moral citizen, failed in marriage, and while achieving all that, seem to have forgotten how to just live and enjoy – but, I *won't* fail us – I mean, our adventure, and I won't let you be harmed. " Though he was honestly of the view that it was Marie who could lend more protection than he.

" No more recriminations, you traitor, you, " grinned Marie warmly. She touched his face, her hand cool and pliant. On a grandiose whim, Thoby cradled her hand and kissed it, as Lancelot would Guinevere.

No one blinked in the station bar; one-night *affaires* so often wound up there.

The mercury in Thoby's psychic meter shot into the stratosphere. They had touched, and it felt superb ! And, his children's crusade was pushing eastward to the alps, clearly favoured by the gods. It would have been over the top to tell Marie, but crammed in his back pocket was a page torn from *The Habsburg Twilight*, a book he'd rolled over to find in the Watts Gallery shed only the morning before. It chronicled the fate of certain Viennese at the turn of the last century, how some had weathered the passage of the empire without docility or suicide. The driving credo of one battered social architect hooked him, and Thoby had borne it off like a tablet from the Mount:

'It is a rare nobility of human nature to change the meanness of defeat into a cause that carries the individual out of his small ego and into humanity.'

(13)

British Andorra's CEC 'Roundtable'
Portsmouth

The *Guardian* had run a hot byte from a corporate ethics guru that morning in an effort to feed off the *Times* tobacco series.

> *'One is left with the inescapable conclusion,*
> *that given the greatest threat to public health this*
> *country has faced since the great plague, people are*
> *having fun making money, and show absolutely no*
> *concern for the consequences of their act.'*

A brief debate amongst the star chamber crew on this scandalous accusation ended with Sir Geoffrey declaiming loudly, and with no apparent connection to its theme, " For Christ's sake, what the hell are people doing smoking brands that are made to be smoked by cowhands and not by the youth of the trendiest, coolest, most 'happening' country in the world ! "

A stiff silence followed.

" ...and speaking of 'consequences', " vaguely reminded he should get on with it, " what to do with this Carlyle bird ?

Prinsep tells me he's singing again. We can absorb that if it's just his 'science' rant – enough out there now it falls on bored ears. But if it's a new shocker – and you can pick your poison – then we ought to consider prompt action. "

" In terms of leverage, his wife's gone and he has no kids… "

" As I said, 'prompt action'. "

" Scuttlebutt has it there's a new woman, a Canadian of some kind…wonder if it's intrigue or lust. "

Trevor Rickerts, NBG director, warmed to the realm of pursuit. " Either way, it makes him more vulnerable. "

" True enough… " Sir Geoffrey leapt in gladly. " Then it's agreed. We – that is, Prinsep and co. – will get the book on this Canuck interloper, but we hang fire until any media eruptions. Our agent has been cautioned not to act prejudicially without specific instruction. "

Hardly a decisive confab, but Sir G. had felt it necessary to 'touch base' (a phrase his secretary urged him to employ) at that moment. Brief meetings made him feel effective, and brevity allowed early exits. It was barely 10:00 a.m., but he had first images of his own inimitable Jeeves (in actuality, an improbable 'Mortimer') proffering his noon elixir.

**

Neale woke early. His eyes popped open like a computer coming on-line, punching the recollected sounds yesterday's conversation between Carlyle and the woman into an uncluttered mind. *'Brookwood...Marie...Lilian...yesterday...cemetery... Nicholson.'* He had only one dream to keep him in bed and it went nowhere until he worked out this hunch. So intent was he on dredging tell-tale data, he stepped into the shower in his shorts. But it was 'Brookwood' that eventually did the trick.

The ever-cheery proprietor of *The Parson's Folly* B&B replied immediately, " Oh, you must mean the *war* graves. Never been myself, but hear it's quite beautiful, very peaceful... "

" Brookwood, Henry Goodfellow speaking… "

Yes, the Chief Custodian recalled, there had been a couple in the Canadian section on the day in question, in the afternoon – hardly a soul that day, not difficult to remember – *no*, no 'Nicholson' plot in that area. But after ten minutes checking the Commonwealth register, there *was* a 'Nichols'. Which was good enough for Neale.

There was no rush now, so Neale went in and had himself a 'full English breakfast', fried bread, tomatoes, and black pudding included – heart seizure on a plate – with a tank of coffee. Then he strolled over to a back-packing shop and bought a collapsible spade and a small hatchet with crow-bar claw...

The modest, red-brick station at Brookwood is a charming throw-back, veiled in ivy, and plunked at the end of a spur line mere minutes out of Woking. A simple path leads out the back towards the memorial grounds. Originally the 'British Military Cemetery', it was first dedicated in 1917 to inter casualties – soldiers, sailors and nurses – who died in London Military District hospitals.

On quiet days, and there aren't many noisy ones in a graveyard, one can hear popping sounds from the rifle range over at Bagshot – a reminder possibly, or a perpetual volley in salute to the dead; but surely no disrespect.

Neale waited on nightfall in a nearby ale house. He used the hours not to speculate on what he might find, as he was very certain of that, but in building courage for a deed even he found unappetizing.

(14)

One minute you're waiting for the sky to fall
The next you're dazzled by the beauty of it all...
Lovers, in a dangerous time

Bruce Cockburn

When seeking an atmospheric 'spy' retreat in which to scheme, romantically or otherwise, the hotel situate at Banhofplatz 11, Bern, is it.

The Gauer family has nurtured the *Schweizerhof* lovingly since 1859. Elegant, tempered architecture, tall interior halls lined with antiques and fine art, the whole fronted with a pedestrian colonnade and serial arches opening on an enclosed square. When Marie and Thoby crossed it, each with their single bag, several old men smoking cheroots and draped in loden capes were pushing half-life-size chessmen around a giant board in the center of the square, intent on their match despite the time of year and gathering dark.

Precisely at 7:00 p.m., as the doorman nodded at the couple entering, an armoured knight glided from the recesses of the great Zytlogge at the far end of the square and smote the bell.

Propitious, noted Thoby, as he opened a memorable *soirée*.

" Guess I was a pawn Marie… "

" A knight Thoby, never forget you're a *knight.* They think they own the board, but you're not playing on it anymore. You've quit the game; *you* can make any move you want – great metaphor isn't it. "

" Well said, faithful advisor ! " What unaccustomed music. " You're going to love it here, if I may say so. Steeped in history. Dynasties and fortunes tumbled here routinely over the last two centuries… "

" We'll do our best to add another victim, " Marie assured her client.

There was no awkwardness about rooms, and Thoby made sure Marie got one with a splendid view of the square and the morning sun.

They descended an hour later to the smaller of two dining rooms, which aped a grand chalet, wood-panelled and very Swiss and cozy in appointments.

Thoby bubbled with reformist zeal, to which Marie played perfect partner. She continued not to miss the practice of law one iota, but the devil in her warmed to the idea of goading a kindred evil.

" So Thoby, if we're 'plotting', what's your… "

" Right, first thing's first, the food here is magnificent. I actually have an appetite, thanks to you. "

Over double gin and tonics, Thoby spilled as many beans to Marie as he'd been able to grab from the B.A. jar before going public. His first sortie had blasted the sham from the industry's much-flogged 'health' research. Undeterred by Fate or worse having dispatched his co-blower, he'd left Somers-Cocks a nice little arsenal: a raft of e.mail orchestrating global smuggling as a mere extension of market strategy. The memos were larded with bodies face-down in Singapore harbour, slumped over wheels in Bogata, and baronets of the realm consorting with Miami thugs. Sure to tickle the readership.

" Then what? " asked Marie, " How do we top that ? Something more 'shocking and appalling', or do we pull the plug on some specific operation you're familiar with ? " She realized she'd neglected to ask the obvious: why they were in Switzerland. She was getting into this nicely, even feeling mildly righteous. She'd left far behind the task of raising arms against a sea of troubles – land mines, dictatorships, atrocities, environmental desecration, domestic violence. It was like leaving a noisy, frenetic bar when she sailed out of Quebec, entering a cool, tranquil backstreet. Here she had the scope to live the romance of Europe, and pick or reject her 'files' – with the poignant mystery of 'Lilian' waiting back across the Channel.

" Some scorchers, salted away at the Bank here, " said Thoby quietly, even *his* enthusiasm hushed by their potential. " Don't know what possessed me at the time, but I had access to records when I subbed on various committees. Stuff that puts the Board clearly in Tehran, Belfast, and Cairo, and *not* as tourists. As handmaidens to terrorism, out-and-out brokers… "

Marie was all-ears. Toby felt a slight rush, as for once in his life, someone close was listening. He'd never felt in control of his marriage or his professional integrity, but here, if the dream didn't get up and leave, there was a perfect echo from one of his beloved western films: 'for the love of a good woman'.

The rest of dinner unfolded luxuriantly amidst stops to be made around Switzerland, France and possibly Belgium. Thoby, now rootless, relished the airy sensation, ready to float anywhere. They laughed and spluttered their way through Black Forest venison and two bottles of cold German white from Bingen. By the time bowls of crème caramel slid onto their table, Thoby was sexually wired and drifting on futuristic seas.

And Marie felt inclined to sail to his rescue. It was ages since she'd had sex, *years* since she'd made love, and Thoby held promise on both accounts; this man with the schoolboy verve and sandy good looks, crying out to communicate and be loved. She respected the quest for personal redemption, rarely displayed by her former clientele.

If they were eventually going to do it on this escapade, *why not now* ? Life is short.

The glowing ambience of the room, a background tapestry with fawns and stags leaping by a stream, the delicious intimacy of plotting sabotage, the chance collision of two complex, vital people from two cultures lent panache, to be sure. They were under a chandelier in a niche of the grand foyer nursing warmed brandy, when Marie stood suddenly and said, " Come up with me, now. I'll show you French Canada. "

Thoby never knew what hit him. Nor for that matter, did Marie, when years of untapped passion and gentle words poured from the whistleblower in torrents.

Somewhere in the middle of the night, she woke when Thoby rolled into her and pleaded, plain as day, " Are you saying my Dad is dead ? There's so much I want to say – I need to see him – he was there, he *was*. That was him whistling. I heard him ! All the birds in the trees. I *saw* him. "

To which Marie's only reaction was a sleepy memory that, technically, she once had a dad herself, and wondered what he'd think of her current situation – *wondered* only, not cared, as he barely constituted a nagging gap in her personal history.

They slept till 10:00 a.m., when they had the promised croissant and café au lait, on silver service, in bed. And wonder of wonders, there was blackcurrant jam for Marie. She didn't even see Thoby slip it from his shaving kit.

It was 2:30 in the afternoon before they wandered into the Banque de Grindelwald.

**

<u>Surrey</u>

If there were fixed criteria of sacrifice for entry into Brookwood Military Cemetery, Sam Neale would have been justly denied; to date, he'd abandoned much and sacrificed nothing. As it was, he simply approached the iron gate and slithered over. A pocket brochure from the train station gave the entire plot grid.

The moon, in Gothic pale, blanched the first row of stones. Momentarily struck by the strange course of his life, Neale thought of the young poet, Lenski, in Tchaikovsky's *Onegin*, and imagined the whistleblower's woman, like Olga, visiting his grave.

An obsession with majestic opera and children's books, however, did not betray a delicate, nor indeed, a literate mind; so it was natural that the sublimity of the now almost incomprehensible dogma in some of the inscriptions entirely eluded Neale as he poked along:

'Know that we fools, now with the foolish dead
Did not for flag, nor King, nor Emperor,
But for a dream, born in a herdsman's shed...'

As for that matter, did the 'beautiful realism' chipped in the slab for one, Marriott-Watson, an 'M' close to 'Nichols', killed in 1918.

'And who is there that believes in Fate
As a soul goes out in the sunset flare'

Neale found Lilian's stone seconds later. He knew it was unlikely, but before anything else, he peeked under the wilted cut flowers and parted the moss around the base in case there was a package of some sort. But there was nothing except cold shadows and a silence that screamed at him, and wouldn't stop until he snapped the spade in place and stabbed it into the short grass over and over.

Neale operated on the assumption that the couple's clandestine meeting at this plot, connected by the word 'documents', meant something of 'tobacco' consequence had been secreted there, though surely at a very shallow depth – how much could they have done in broad daylight ? He scraped away a rectangle about five feet by three, and six inches deep, uncovering nothing but a George V penny.

A light sweat developed with his labour, and the fearsome quiet no longer registered. It seemed absurd, but here he was, and he might as well do a thorough job. What did the English say, 'in for a penny, in for a pound' ? So Neale dug up the ambulance driver's coffin.

It consumed three full hours, more manual work than Neale had performed in his entire life, and the net gain, when he clawed apart the pulpy remnants of the box, was a piece of mouldy paper almost floating inside the clasped hands. He refused to confront the face, looking instead around the periphery for sinister objects, again without success.

The paper unfolded without tearing, spilling a tuft of ribbon-bound, chestnut hair. The hand-inked words were frighteningly legible,

> *'My dearest heart, you pulled him from the path of harm, so here is a part of him which will be with you for all time'*

> *Neale regarded his little find for some minutes, turning the sheaf over and over as if some material revelation would flutter out. At length, he realized he hadn't found what he expected and transferred that failure as more hostility towards Carlyle.*

His infatuation with Marie quelled the reflex to toss the note. At the same time, it occurred that what he held might be valuable. Perhaps there was a connection between the two women, despite the huge gap in years. He decided to preserve the piece of paper and the hair, and find a way to present it, find a way to impress her – look at the effort he'd already made on her behalf ! Of course, now he'd have to eliminate Carlyle.

Like a dog instinctively pawing dirt in the general direction of its droppings, Neale kicked a few scoops of earth back into the hole, dropped the spade in, and walked away.

**

Grindelwald,
der Steinadler

Marie decided to make a quick call to London while their waiter set up the fondue equipment.

She'd nearly forgotten, especially after a full day hiking from Wengen up to Kleine Scheidegg, in the glacial face of the great trinity of the Bernese Oberland: the *Eiger*, *Mönch* and *Jungfrau*. That afternoon, she'd burst shamelessly into the Sound of Music as they floated down the other side several kilometers to Grindelwald, into green, pastoral landscapes.

" Chelsea Constabulary, P/C Witherspoon… "

" Yes, is Constable Dove there please ? It's the Canadian from the Cheyne Row break-in… "

" She's not on at the moment ma'am, but maybe I can be of assistance…did the follow-up on that one actually. Nabbed the other bloke pretty quick, if that's what you're after – the pair of them well-known rounders. Been doin' the area for some time, they had…'

" I see. Do you know if anything further was recovered, I… "

" Not a thing. Usual situation, I'm afraid… "

" Well…thanks very much then. "

So, there was no link between Thoby and her loss; it deflated physical apprehensions in joining his merry band. Could his own risk perception have then been over-estimated ? Yet native curiosity quickly filled the void: wasn't her whole drift to spontaneity ? If she hadn't gone, he'd be out there alone and she'd never learn the outcome.

The rosy glow of a flourishing intimacy wasn't to be overlooked either...

Thoby brought a copy of the *Times* to breakfast at their small Interlaken hotel. The page-two story ran under the banner, '**British Andorra In Bed With Smugglers**'. Several senior officers, including a baronet, were patently skewered, and would almost certainly be hung out to dry by the company, but for some reason, Thoby was not elated.

" Aren't you pleased they ran it ? "

" Should be front page…and there's no government response. They're all in the same trough, hand in glove…I'll call again today, *insist* that Irish stuff we scooped gets out. "

Marie and Thoby agreed that more effective avenues lay back in England, and their 'inaugural' tour should end for the moment, though two 'must-do's remained.

The first involved bolting directly for Paris. Marie had her day in the Louvre, and the late afternoon seated in the Jardin des Tuilleries, imagining herself as a coquette in an Impressionist tableau. They stayed in the 5ieme Arrondissement, in a piquant hotel in the Place Monge, and paid a small fortune for an exquisite dinner somewhere along the Champs.

The other essential emerged from Marie's phone call. The reminder of the young ambulance driver and her letters compelled a mini-pilgrimage.

" We *have* to visit Ypres, Thoby. Don't you agree, put a special stamp on our meeting one another ? "

" Spot on Marie, but why exactly…? "

" Lilian rescued Joseph at Passchendaele, remember ? Only the other day in the *Herald Tribune* I read the town still holds a *daily* sunset ceremony. Thoby ! What a thing to be there, as close as I'll ever get to Joseph and Lilian… "

Two hours later, they were on a high-speed train crossing into Belgium, Thoby the slave to Marie's dynamic urging. The weather held crystal-clear till twilight, when the pair strolled with a surprising crowd of at least a 1000 towards Menin Gate.

There wasn't a martial bone in her body, yet Marie shivered when buglers from Ypres blew the *Last Post* at precisely 8:00 p.m. Lines from Owen and Sassoon sighed heavily in the cold air, and as with her experience at Brookwood, many of '*the unreturning army that was youth*' seemed to press in shoulder to shoulder for the occasion.

They both remarked on the hushed tone of those present and visible. At one point, Thoby, chastened by the emotional venue, turned away in tears after conscience summoned the army of youngsters *he* might have rescued.

They drifted afterwards in silence to a small *brasserie*. They shared a huge plate of *frites* and a bottle of *Château Timberlay*, feeling spoiled indeed to be alive in the 21st century and indulging themselves. Marie looked up suddenly and smiled.

" Thank you for coming here Thoby… "

" My sweet woman… a pittance of time to spend, a pittance… "

They looked at each other and understood that for themselves, as for the last stragglers past the window, there were a myriad motives for coming, but they all had cared, and come.

**

Somers-Cocks engineered Thoby's 'Irish' goodies onto the front page of the next edition of the *Times*. He scored extra with a global update on '**Big Tobacco Deflowered**' in the weekend magazine. The most lurid revelation was of B.A.'s joint enterprise in the early 90's with the Ulster Defence Alliance, the virulent northern Ireland paramilitary.

The UDA mob had routinely levied 'punishment' killings on gang rivals and even their own colleagues in counterfeit, prostitution, and cigarette smuggling. In 1995, they succeeded in inadvertently murdering two of B.A.'s regional managers in a Surrey pub blast. A British public, however, bruised and paranoid from years of IRA terror, racial violence, and random skinhead lobotomy, absorbed the latest industry shenanigans with remarkable poise, if not indifference.

Not so Sir Geoff. Corporate wisdom decreed a threshold had been reached, a line fatally traversed. It was imperative that the wandering mouth now be shut, permanently, before partners and competitors questioned B.A.'s viability. And so the word, *sub rosa*, went out.

" Prinsep, let loose your dog. And make sure he cleans up after… "

Neale turned duly ravenous, keen to be operative; moreover, it gave legitimacy to pursuing the woman.

So far, though, frustration had been the lousy return on his Swiss feelers. With the lock of hair and notepaper in hand, Neale felt like the wallflower alone with her corsage at a dance. *Yes*, they'd entered, but hadn't shown themselves in Geneva – half-hour visit to a bank in Bern, but apparently took only 500 Euros – and their few sightings elsewhere revealed no pattern before exiting to France.

Neale had easily acquired Marie's name by dropping in on Marita the day after the break-in, to 'double-check on any missing personal property'; Marita, with divine prudence, had said Marie was a Canadian niece with the same last name, 'Clarke'. No credit cards had been used, and who knew what names they sheltered under at night. The issue was when and where they would return. It would take work, but the notch-up in excitement meshed well with that of the pending opera season.

Tennyson's Cross, I.O.W.
Christopher McNaught
2001

(15)

Have you news of my boy Jack ?
Not this tide
When do you think that he'll come back ?
Not with this wind blowing, and this tide
Kipling

The High Down, Freshwater Bay
Isle of Wight,
May, 1919

Charlotte Nichols unbuttoned her long cardigan and the neck of her blouse. She was breathing freely, invigorated by her climb towards 'Tennyson's Cross' on the crest of the Down. The entire sky was a pastiche of slip-stream cloud, and the swathes of colour tinting the sea out to her left – turquoise, cobalt, mauve – were washed and lifted by a giant paintbrush. For the first time since March, she felt herself edging beyond mere desolation, into an uncharted peace. It was almost uncanny how grief dissipated into an infinite ceiling.

Her journey to the south shore of Wight had proven fruitless. Not that intuition had warned otherwise, but there could be no solace for a mother in not coming. Months of dogging Canadian and Imperial authorities had produced achingly little;

at times she suspected they were annoyed by her inquiries, as if she ought to have been ashamed to ask, and desisted. All they permitted her to see was an army clerk's marginal notation in November, 1917, beside the name, '*J. Herbert* (misspelled)... *court-martial pending*: *transferred to Dimbola Lodge, IOW, for custodial treatment (mental)*'. No end-date, no description of charges, no record anywhere of what afterwards became of her Joseph.

And thus Charlotte came to Freshwater with meager expectation, if only to be physically proximate to his final days.

As she approached the mammoth Celtic cross, the sun burst through along the cliff-top from east to west, bathing her with invisible balm. Char read the inscription:

TENNYSON
1809 – 1892

In memory of Alfred Lord Tennyson
This cross is raised, a beacon to sailors by the people of
Freshwater & other Friends in England and America

In her half-mournful, half-euphoric state, she could retrieve only a single line of Tennyson from school days, and that surfaced because of the word 'sailors', and recollecting the poem had something to do with a boy going off to sea against family wishes: '*He heard a fierce mermaiden cry...I see the place where thou wilt lie*'. Then she had to settle gratefully on the ocean-side bench to rest and absorb the panorama.

Three fishing smacks dotted the lazy-seeming swell out toward the horizon. The air, clean and gloriously silent, except for the odd gull wheeling dizzily off the cliff-face to remind one of the inability to fly, did everything but caress her. She unlaced her boots and squiggled her toes in the spungy growth covering the chalk; the rich green ran on like a vast carpet another kilometer to drop from the 'Needles' into Alum Bay at the west tip of Wight. *Sain foin*, primrose, and heather streaked the carpet crimson and purple. Dwarf roses and lady fingers laced the fringes. In minutes, she was nodding to herself. *Up here – oh my soul ! Up here is how life should have been…*

For a chill instant, her gaze strayed beyond the sea and the moment, back to René's grave on the bare hill at Lévis – but it would be absurd to cry in this rare place, and in any event, her well of tears had long since run dry.

The past two days had been a desolate roller coaster. Char had located *Dimbola* easily enough, but discovered it had changed hands and no record survived of any 'brave boys' spending convalescence behind its friendly windows. Of no consolation was the cruel morsel gleaned from two spinsters guiding each other along the sea-wall, that *several* Canadians had in fact 'stayed on' to marry local girls shortly after the Armistice.

On the same afternoon, trailing up from Terrace Lane and her dashed hopes at *Dimbola*, Char had entered Orchard Bros., the venerable provisioner at the fork leading to *Farringford*. She'd ignored the papers which obsessed with war reparations and Spanish influenza, and bought some stick-candy and a bottle of Porter for her room at the *Albion*. She also acquired, gratuitously, a first-hand account of *Dimbola*'s role in 19th century letters from the 60 year-old proprietress, Lizzie Troubridge.

Char was a voracious reader, mind you; imagination's windows had offered comfort in her early brush with the New World. When Lil eventually leapt into the chaos and left her in unbearable solitude at her parents' cottage in Surrey, to preserve sanity, she had devoured all her archdeacon-father's tomes on history, philosophy, and religion. Her own hardship in South Africa and Quebec lent a bitter, informed perspective on the times, which was to say, the folly of men. She was thus *au courant*, and, in the realm of artistic vogue for example, relatively open-minded towards such 'radical' challengers of cant and turgid Imperial hype as the 'Bloomsberries', the abrasive clique then tweaking London tongues. She was, though, unfamiliar with that group's tangled geneology, and now learned how ignorant she'd been of the high-voltage legacy tumbling off the Down directly behind her.

Lizzie Troubridge informed Char of how, at the age of 5, a stout tempest of a woman had regularly blown without warning from the hedges to whisk her off the Lane, into bizarre apparel, then pose her at agonizing length, often with total strangers, in front of a mysterious box. At various times, she'd been styled as waif or angel, but was best-known in a now-famous photograph as '*Virginie*'.

Lizzie, for whom the parish at Freshwater became her universe, grew to know her abductor as the indomitable *salonnière* and portraitist, Julia Cameron. She developed a reverence for 'Mrs. C.', as she called her, appreciating in retrospect her demonic energy, and how unfailingly couched it was in warmth and inspiration.

Cameron's disregard for the rigid poses of early photography irked some, but her quest to 'capture' the fleshly signs of inner greatness at her Lodge on Wight during the'60's and'70's stirred a cream-pot of Victorian writers, artists, poets and philosophers. And of these, none capitulated more charismatically to her task of rendering 'beauty' than her neighbour, Alfred Tennyson.

According to Lizzie, the bard and Cameron, separately driven, had forged a rough mutual affinity which catalysed in at least one joint venture; though in that enigmatic union, Cameron operated more as patroness, and he, bedeviled beneficiary. 'Mrs. C. was forever pointing out his *sage eyes* and *noble brow'* – Char glanced up at the yellowed Cameron print of the poet Laureate peering studiously over the chemist shelves and thought: *baggy-eyed and balding.*

When so inclined, or more often, when 'summoned', Tennyson routinely headed down on a path leading directly from his *Farringford* estate to access *Dimbola* by a gate specially constructed for him at the rear, away from the plague of admirers – 'it's still there dear, you *must* walk through it once'. He would appear in dramatic cape and broad-rimmed hat for all-season walks onto the Down with Cameron, and sometimes young Anny Thackeray, or promenades to the *Albion* and the sea-wall for a 'genial hour of pipe and grog', stormy weather preferred. On summer evenings, subject to his wife Emily's health, he would attend impromptu concerts or *soirées* contrived by Cameron with *Dimbola*'s current guests – complete with her hand-drawn programs.

The Lord – 'he loathed that you know, after he finally accepted his peerage, insisted on *Mr. and Mrs. T.*' – would rush into Orchard Bros. at odd hours to purchase tobacco. 'He was putty in Mrs. C.'s hands...I do treasure my copy of *Idylls of the King* – she illustrated it, you see…after the Camerons sailed back to Ceylon she wrote him and had one of his sons deliver a signed copy to me – she insisted on that, though between you and me, I was thrilled just to *know* her'.

This lore was charming, her own misery notwithstanding; and only months later, when Char consented to tea in London with her publishing cousin, she learned that Virginia Woolf, of Strachey and Keynes notoriety, was in fact the great-niece of none other than 'Mrs. C.', and the daughter of the subject of arguably her most soulful and enduring portrait.

But Char had not bridged the Solent as admiring pilgrim.

It was now, after all, plain that her pitiful journey ended here, at the cliff-edge, her brief torch extinguished by the lovely gossamer dancing on the summit.

She'd failed, and the only next step lay before her…

**

A kilometer down and to the east of Charlotte, on the other hand, Gerald Brenan, late of the 5th Gloucesters, was finding much of what he sought.

Planted knee-deep and motionless in Freshwater Bay, he stared trance-like over the incoming tide, convinced that not moving would assure re-entry into life beyond the slough. The cold water would freeze what he'd seen and done in Flanders, then slide it out and away beneath the flow, scourged, cleansed, removed forever. In short order, validating this notional process, the surge and pull began to feel warm around his calves. A fresh, salt-stung harmony tingled from between his toes into the beach reshaping itself, the surf rhythmically collapsing, the Bay's enfolding pinnacles, all the way out to the Dutchman's sky.

There was no elation. Any kind of serenity composed itself well out of present sight; at best, there was a gradual resuscitation from prolonged deadening of emotion.

The waves, particularly, held Brenan mesmerized. No matted skulls lay pressed in the sand, no bloody rivers leaked from 16 year-old fodder. The rollers broke on the pebbles without random, cataclysmic hell, in lovely falls and a clean backwash of marble and turquoise, making a pleasant 'sa-*loosh*'.

After a half hour or so listening, he clearly heard them beckon, 'Anda-*lu*sia, Anda-*lu*sia'. Their resonance grew with every gentle repetition…*south of Grenada maybe.* Dry, open, a colourful sanctuary, a land unscathed by carnage and *détente*, a place in which to refit curiosity, possibly uncover evidence of humanity before the storm…yes, *Spain !*

" 'Spain' ? Surely one can't see it from here ! "

The captain flinched, then turned slowly. An older woman – he'd wheedled Death into granting his 25th birthday – skirt hiked nonchalantly to mid-thigh, stood near him in the foam. So close in fact, they might have been wedged together in a Piccadilly bus. She was flushed, and a little short of breath.

In the penultimate second, Char had found a way back from the precipice: *someone must survive; otherwise, my loss is meaningless, our passage unrecorded.* She reconciled herself to a future, however empty, and flustered by that prospect, had hurtled non-stop all the way down to the Bay. The young man alone at the brink of the sea had embodied peace and calm, and she had gravitated unconsciously to his shelter.

" Damn ! Babbling again, Gerald... "

" ...apologize – Oh, *so sorry* ! So silent we were, then your voice startled me. I took you literally, out of context I'm sure – presumptuous of me...taken off my boots as you can see. It *does* feel wonderful on the legs ! "

" Hm-hmm... "

The breeze continued in friskily off the Channel, devoid of gas and putrefaction. An immense world brimmed out there, with shifting hues and marvelous denizens – the holy miracle of creation, made more miraculous by his having survived in its embrace.

Brenan struggled with the moment: it was painful expunging personal agonies from the elements, difficult recalling that other humans too, could be worthwhile, and not just hate-crazed mongerers. But Char did not annoy him – her presence in some way was not intrusive. At length, he extended a genuine arm around her shoulders, in case she tottered.

" Are you quite alright, then ? ", he offered.

" Yes, quite...*winded*, thanks. Not myself... "

" I suspect this air could heal anything. " *Another wounded soul.* " Tennyson said he'd pay *6p* anytime just for a breath of it...walked the place over nearly every day I'm told. "

Culture and solicitude...Char turned to face her protector. An officer, clearly. She recognized the bearing and the melancholy, the intense eyes clouded by terrible things. His thick hair was honey-coloured and crop-cut, and a worn red kerchief was knotted above the neck of a cream Irish jumper. A tight, well-drawn mouth looked poised to reflect on life, if only freed to do so. In her quick judgment, this was a cultivated, spirited boy who'd been hushed by God-knew-what.

" You were over there weren't you... " Another, almost imperceptible flinch of the right eye. " Do forgive me – the war has led me here as well. Seeking answers – we all are, aren't we...I suppose ? "

Char took his quizzical smile and silence as affirmation. She continued softly, though the only living thing within 200 meters was a German shepherd vainly chasing sandpipers to the water-line.

" *My* search has died, however. I accept that; no more clues... " She looked carefully out to sea to distance Brenan from what she was saying. " One hears idiot fathers parading about, bragging how proud they are 'to have given a son to my country', but no one will tell me what happened to *mine* – I hadn't even the opportunity to 'give' him up... "

The poor man, Char, enough.

" Probably heard a thousand tales like mine – then of course, *you* must be someone's son, happily returned… "

She regretted instantly the word 'happily', so insensitive.

Brenan bent closer to the lustrous eyes and Grecian features, their attitude tenderly resigned like a *pietà*. There was a true bell ringing, but he was uncertain why. Maybe it was the eerie likeness to a photo his friend Ralph Partridge had shown him a week ago on the Woolfs' coffee table in London. The woman gazing beyond the frame had set him off on several hopelessly affected poems. Or maybe it was just the first statue he'd seen intact amid the ruins. But there was beauty here, resilient in circumstance…

" No fear madam, I am without question 'returned' – however cold the home-fires – and 'happy' I am to be, if only to stir the ashes… " As for 'someone's son', his military father had all but whined at his not being killed or disfigured. He'd already tried to shove a remote Indian Army posting down the now-apostate Brenan's craw, as if a life of brutality was just what the field surgeon had ordered…

But it *was* therapeutic, picking up again. All the magic threads. How precious, life, how thrilling to indulge the aesthetic. Here he stood, invoking Tennyson in his own backyard, recalling Cameron portraits only a green field from her *Lodge*. Ah Freshwater, thou once and vital enclave ! Another, *creative* time, driven by grand principle yet dancing on the edge. Most of its gentle pioneers had passed before the August guns; surely their spirits wept at the apocalyptic madness…

Brenan teetered, drifting off the beach into the mystical: an innate habit. Mysticism had been his faithful ally in evading the slough, evicting insanity and stoking survival. Invalided back to England just prior to the Armistice, he was appalled at the chauvinist blather choking the country's papers; the excess and vulgarity he saw tainting the green and pleasant land hemmed him in, and now compelled an exit, spiritually and physically. It seemed ironic, sad, that in order to re-integrate, to breathe freely, he should need to leave again. And even so, Iberia called.

The breeze shifted suddenly, sending Char's unbound hair into a flurry of tresses, and a wisp of something elegant and faded caught Brenan's nostrils. It was haunting: a Paris furlough, but couldn't remember if it was in a shop, or a passing girl, *Blue*-something…

But this held Char in his focus. How rude, not right to be so distracted. *This anguished soul beside me on the strand, are we the last two caring*…a poem here, but not now Gerald. The lovely woman appeared free of the rabid yowl for hanging all Germans, Irishmen and 'conscies'. He could muster kindness on a one-to-one basis. His native interest in the human condition prevailed; it was in him to approach the individual in a scene…

" It would be a pleasure, indeed an honour, if you would join me for a cream tea. I'm staying with a painter-friend in Dorset and am just here for a day or two. I dare say we have much in common and both could use some company, if not dry feet… "

Char nodded, with the ghost of a smile she'd forgotten she possessed.

They walked silently up to the seawall and sat against it, methodically brushing the sand from their feet in the warm sun. Then Brenan stood and crooked his arm to escort Charlotte Nichols to the west end of the cove and the *Albion*'s front terrace.

" Please tell me more about your search ... "

Now and then along life's pathway,
Lo ! Some shining pieces fall;
But there are so many pieces
No one ever finds them all

Priscilla Leonard

The raisin scones came fresh from the oven, surrounding a pot of jam exploding with fruit, and watercress sandwiches prettily arranged in wild mockery of trench-life. Brenan still boggled at the luxury of china and multiple utensils. He approached such fare as if a feast to which he was unentitled, savouring every drop and crumb – and that he should sit down to it against a sparkling, backdrop sea !

Char poured freely, from the teapot and her heart. The rapport between mother and officer was immediate and unspoken, aided by collective loss and poetic sensibility. Out spilled the peculiar history of the twins, their separation and unknowing reunion at Passchendaele, ending in Char's double bereavement. Even amidst the twisted wreckage that formed his war memory, Brenan was shaken.

" …and they – *gracious* ! I don't know your name yet, aren't we risqué ! "

" 'Brenan, Gerald Brenan', and you are perceptive, I was a captain… "

" Well then, Cap… "

" 'Gerald', please, dear…? "

" 'Charlotte Nichols', and do please call me anything but 'Lottie'. " The repetition of Brenan's name made her pause for an instant, then she continued. " …they sent Lilian two medals after she died – what ever would I want with them ? Of course I'm proud – at her age, it was a pure and ignorant sacrifice – but she didn't seek them and they won't bring her back to me. The metal's only cold weight on her wasted body… " and then her composure failed.

Brenan was proud too, of his *Military Cross* and *Croix de Guerre*, but only in a deep personal recess. On the public parade ground, the indifferent will for closure, and the hate-the-Hun, never-make-peace propaganda revolted him and sullied his 'gongs'. *For King and…?* Already that year, Kipling, the Imperial cheerleader himself, his son blown to bits and lost at Loos, had written, '*If any question why we died, tell them because our fathers lied* '.

But the tea was soothing, and steeped in Char's engaging aura. The moment begged a brighter turn.

" Permit me to attest that the ambulance people I observed carried out perilous duty. I hold profound awe and admiration for their valour…ever-cheerful, slogging to the utmost in godless conditions. You have every right and obligation to be proud of your daughter – and your son – no matter the civilian lunatics. "

" ...so very kind Cap...Gerald. "

" Let me add without shame, those of us still above ground in the final months, Fritz included, committed to one flag and one flag alone: survival. Blood-lust had died, we were sick in heart and mind and body. We dreamed of home... "

And here he was, prepared so soon to abandon it...he wondered if he should ask more about the son, but Char had circled back.

If Jo had longed for 'home', it couldn't have been the Surrey room preserved on faith he'd just walk in one day. Char grew agitated and stood abruptly, looking seaward.

" No medals came for Joseph. They didn't know I existed, nor did he for pity's sake – I've nothing left of him. A too-short infancy, years tormented by not sharing his passages... " Char reached blankly into her large sweater pocket. " All's left is this shred of paper... " which she held out for the world in general.

" May I... " Brenan rose gently from his chair, cradled one hand under hers and waited patiently till she let go.

The single leaf had a hole worn at the center fold, and a blackish-red smeared the pencil script in two places. He froze directly he started reading, recognizing it. Years up the line had immobilized overt reaction, so he didn't budge for minutes, causing Char to lean forward anxiously. Then a second impulse made her snatch back the page.

She held it with both hands and read it out loud, deliberately, to make very sure:

To commemorate reflections with a fine Canadian colleague, in the slough at Passchendaele,

November 5, 1917
Gerald Brenan

Into the valley they rode, and rode, and rode…

Char mouthed the signature over and over – not for the sound, but to secure to her heart the irrefutable link. This Captain Brenan, her tea partner, had met and conversed with *her* Joseph in the thunder of war; he'd even memorialized the fact ! Didn't this show how fine her boy was ? Her time at Freshwater now seemed pre-ordained.

Brenan was stunned that he'd even known the date at the time. Char would examine and cross-examine him on every nuance of that distant, brief encounter. He worried how to relate what now became a precious locket of remembrance…

" You…*you're* the 'Ger…' "

" Yes, incredibly… "

A rogue breaker died on the rocks below the terrace, spraying the pair, but Char only stared, her features paralysed in a beautiful mist.

The lad alone at the parapet, shivering in a kilt – *the Gallic and the Gaelic* – he remembered the occasion now vividly, quiet and other-worldish. And the note, marking the shaky emergence of his muse from the mire of Ypres.

Char hardly had voice to implore him.

" What was he like? What did he say ? Was he handsome like his father – but you'd not know that. Was he alright then, not hurt – oh *please*, what did he *say* ? "

Even as he grappled with his own amazement, Brenan girded for a performance. " It seems Fate has honoured me as messenger with news of your son. My honest recollection is of a very striking young man ('boy' was the fact, but why accent the heartbreak), dark eyes, dark hair, with full grasp of his situation, fortitude itself. He was quite intact when I spoke with him. I recall we traded memories of our favourite prospects – his at Quebec I believe, and mine, here… "

" Did he mention 'home' or speak of…a 'mother' ? "

She had to ask that, but Brenan found it excruciating keeping his eyes on hers.

" One never dwelt on such things out there Charlotte, particularly before a big offensive. Now I think of it, I confess to a strange sort of bond with him, which is why I never asked his name – you didn't wish to know those you might lose at any instant – we shook hands and that was it… "

They both sat down, emotionally drained. Char was still agitated but knew instinctively there was nothing more to be recovered. The little note rested amid the remnants of the cream tea like a spent, dud shell.

Brenan pulled a copy of the *Times* from his haversack.

" Believe it or not Charlotte, " he began, scanning the banner leads for support, " the gods envy us. *Our* loves and losses come once only; *they* are condemned to eternal re-enactment, Promethean cycles. Don't you see, everything we feel or chance upon in life happens then, and never again, en route to our mortality. Why do we fritter away that unique gift, blowing each other up for horrors we jointly caused, or wander about, seeking some saving grace… "

Char was vulnerable and ready to go with the tide towards a different hope.

" …when we can *exult* in our lot ? We have that choice. We can be worms in the trench muck, oozing guilt and retribution – look here… " and Brenan slid the paper over to Char with his finger on the center story:

Versailles, May 15, 1919
from our Special correspondent

Count Brockdorff-Rantzan Issues
Economic Commission Report on Effect
of Peace Terms

Under the terms of the treaty Germany is to give
up her Merchant Marine and vessels now under
construction suitable for foreign commerce...
Moreover, Germany must renounce her colonies…

" …or we can soar above it all, like…like Icarus refurbished, free of the gods ! " And he pointed triumphantly to the photo and fanfare above the right-hand column:

American Navy Seaplane Flies Atlantic
" NC-4 " Bounces off Azores into History…

" Truly Gerald, you're leaking Irish. I believe you'd save the lost men returned from France. I don't know how you did it, but I feel…*inspired* even. This bay, the air, its ghosts, helped I'm sure, but I do believe I thank you… "

" Not me at all dear lady, the sky – so blue, so kind – we can lift our hearts up to that. Funny, standing in the sand this afternoon, I fetched up my childhood and it occurred to me that we don't have to abandon that joy; there are castles inside us which we can always build and re-shape… "

" You mentioned the great poet earlier; only yesterday someone I met was on about him – this is his haunt after all. Now I've roamed the ground and watched the waves – don't think me mawkish – I understand why he shared his gloom and sorrow with the elements; they took them in, freed his spirit …you and I've done just that today, haven't we ? Immersed ourselves… "

Brenan let the very last of the tea trickle down his throat, loathe to end the event, yet tugging inside to set sail for his newer world. Typically, he was already casting the day in tight lines: *souls lost, remembered, and mended, by the beauty of their lust for life…*

" Indeed we have, shared a great deal more than sweets. As survivors, we verge on being, I dare say, a little family… "

Char looked gratefully across the table at her handsome companion, blushing slightly.

" You remind me so of my dear René...may you have many happy adventures in your life...Would you care for a stroll, walk me back into the village ? "

On their way up past Terrace Lane, both peeked in at *Dimbola*, each with different sentiments. When they reached the fork, Char steered Brenan into the Orchard Bros. shop.

" Miss Troubridge, this is Captain Brenan. He's wonderfully familiar with the people you described for me yesterday... " As a result of which, Lizzie and Brenan traded gems mapping the spiritual and 'Bohemian' origins of Bloomsbury back to the 'Freshwater Circle' for some time. Lizzie knew little if nothing about London salons, *avant garde* or not, while the reluctant prodigal from Flanders rejoiced in hearing, first-hand, of Tennyson flying kites with his sons on the Down.

Char happened on '*Mrs. Herbert Duckworth*' in a cardboard bin of photos and old 'cartes de visite' beside the register. With Brenan's keen approval, she bought the inspired immortalization of Virginia Woolf's mother. *Something tangible...* Till the end of her life, Char paid daily homage to the grace and regality of Cameron's break-the-mould composite of woman, the pure beauty of which captured Char's longings on that May day.

They parted at the door of '*Myrtle Cottage*', where Char was billeted, with a bold, heartfelt kiss on Brenan's cheeks, knowing their pathes would never cross again.

Brenan sauntered back to the *Albion*, pensive and revitalized. Under one arm was a used anthology of Tennyson, courtesy of a charmed Miss Troubridge. After bangers and mash and a pint of *Smithwicks*, he sat out on his balcony to commune again with the ocean. He watched the small boys race about till cornered by nannies, and the night fishermen set their line and plant their tot of whisky within easy reach. A great sigh rolled from the land onto the water, and he felt agreeably heavy with caring and all things beautiful.

He drifted off somewhere amongst *The Lotus-Eaters*:

'...tir'd lids upon tir'd eyes
Music that brings sweet sleep down from blissful skies
Here are cool mosses deep
And thro' the mosses the ivies creep,
And in the stream the long-leaved flowers weep,
And from the craggy ledge the poppy hangs in sleep'

(16)

And all I ask is a tall ship and a star to steer her by...

It was Advent. When the English flee to Spain, Majorca, and the Caribbean.

Not so Sam Neale. A Christmas tour of the world's great tenors and divas was set to electrify concert halls and special venues throughout the U.K. The Nativity was therefore a non-event for Sam, though it did bring a surfeit of children's books to browse.

The woman clearly duped by Carlyle had thereafter dominated Neale's bare and sordid stage; only the lust and delusion of such a raw ego could challenge his mania for soaring arias. That said, locating this 'Marie Clarke' and saving her from a second-rate affaire had to be a more or less immediate achievement, as any doubt in her whereabouts or itinerary would in the short term be resolved in favour of fixed recitals – British Andorra and Prinsep be damned.

**

December 20,
Boulogne sur Mer

Freidrich Rüpp was a happy man. His daughter was studying at the Institut d'Études Politiques in Lille and he'd come from Davos to 'rescue' her from the grey and damp of *le nord*. 'Let's take a chance the coast will be sunny' he'd urged, and when their train shot out of the morning mist above Boulogne, it had been, gloriously.

A long walk along the beach together towards the far Cap, with stick drawings in the powder-sand and wading up to the knees, then back over the seawall to purchase huge baguettes and two large bottles of *Affligem Bière de Noel* – a Swiss bureaucrat genetically enslaved to tradition, Rüpp was delighted to hear the latter was still brewed exclusively by monks, as it had been since 1074. They scaled the cliffs rising behind the shops and cafés to picnic in the extraordinarily mild afternoon, seated on an overgrown German pillbox; an elderly woman walking her spaniel informed them the Canadians had liberated that stretch.

When a low train of cloud quit the northwestern horizon, Bluette exclaimed at the faint saffron-white left daubing the sea, " *Schau Vater, dass muss England sein !* "

Rüpp squinted dutifully. His mouth opened to confirm that what she spied was indeed the native shore of hooligans, suspect social programs, and mongrel hordes in general, when a couple speaking English appeared a few feet to his right.

" There Marie, *there* she is ! " Thoby was excited; he was returning a changed man; maybe not a king, but the sceptered isle could very well be welcoming a new prince… “ Imagine standing here in 1942, scrounging for bread but able to *see* freedom just over the water… ”

“ Imagine what British Andorra would think if they knew *we* were about to invade ! ” and they hooted in unison, coming ‘home’ together for the first time. Marie’s eyes already looked beyond the white cliffs, canvassing an adventure without tobacco stains.

Rüpp’s head snapped around. He could hardly believe it. The alarm bells of a senior customs agent rang loud and clear: trained instinct ignores time and place; it simply works when stimulated. He waited till the pair meandered along further towards the Napoleonic block house, then flipped open his cell phone.

“ Yeah… ”

“ Samuel ? ”

“ Yeah… ”

“ Iss Freidrich hehr – zay are hehr, in France ! Ze two persons you vished to find ! Right beside me… ”

“ Where’s ‘in France’, where *are* you ? ”

“ Boulogne. Ve are lookink now at you, at England… ”

“ You’re sure… ”

“ Ze man called ze woman ‘Marie’, and zay both laughed ven she said ‘British Andorra’…yah, she *iss* very attractive, yah… ”

Neale strayed unusually close to actual politesse.

" Bingo ! A miracle...*danke*, Freddy, saved my bacon... "

" Vass is... "

" Nothing – hey, maybe we'll see each other soon and I can thank you with Champagne. " Flat emotions exhausted, he moved abruptly to the next item. " You saw von Otter will be on the Isle of Wight next week – you got the notice, eh ? "

Neale's mobile had an asterisk beside Rüpp's name. In addition to being a key border official, he was also an insane opera buff, equally compelling values in Neale's world. Both men were on the 'Gold Circle' e.mail distribution list for European opera promotions.

It seemed logical to Neale, given their present location, and the now-determined fact they'd not flown or taken the *Eurostar* on the way out, that they would simply proceed to Calais, a stone's throw above Boulogne, and take the ferry. Doubtless an amateur effort at low-profile movement...it would be easy to get someone to mind the ferry traffic at the English end. He made a note to forward the photos and message already sent to Geneva to Calais and Dover, including the Hoverspeed and P&O Ferries people.

Christ ! With any luck, in a few days he'd have popped Carlyle and be guiding Marie through a dramatic evening of music and superior sex...he'd impress the hell out of her !

**

She hadn't mooted it about thoroughly with him, but now they were headed back, Marie felt strongly that Thoby's investment in revisionism should shift from the global to the self. 'You rattled their cage, turned the media onto their fraudulent campaigns and cash-cow greed. And yes, you've renounced *your* past – but Thoby, it's time to move on from *mea culpa* – no more flagellation, *mon cher*. You're not indelibly branded, or worthless; you've new worlds to conquer, joy to find…' She preached as well to her own new needs.

She'd weighed the pros and cons of 'Thoby' and found little in the latter column to deter. Mysteriously, Marie had entered the confessional, where, despite mile after sweaty mile of running to forget, and violent oaths she'd never slip again, she had to admit liking the smell of his jacket, his skin, the crush of his arms, and the Robin Hood-Tom Sawyer world he so plainly sought to restore. She was prepared – no, *longed* – to join that Sherwood band, climb onto the raft. Not as a mere camp-follower, but as co-voyager, life-mate. They could drop career mantles and 'go forth' – *for Pete's sake, Marie, you've become a 'muscular Christian'!* – kindred spirits, into a consuming partnership, something unique. They had the brains, the raw funds, and the love to do it.

Life, as several of Marie's former clients' victims had discovered, is short, and the meter on the vital allotment she now chose to bestow on this Englishman was already running. She was cynic enough for the two of them to gauge how quickly the media-crazed public tired of crusaders, of 'insider' celebs.

From Marie's view as counselor and lover, Thoby couldn't re-invent himself too soon.

'...you're more use to people if you're happy, engaged; you can wave *any* sword you want. You know Thoby, I was thinking, why not absolve our childless lives by collaborating on a series of kids books, create fresh 'classics'? Maybe a disabled science nerd who skirmishes with the mega-corps, or a school-girl fighting sectarian shackles, a kind of older *Madeleine* or *Eloise* with attitude...or *maybe*, our dear Lilian: *Daughter of the Great War*? Come on, let's do it!' Marie picked up the pieces and was, typically, gung-ho to gain advantage from them...

Quite different, the perspective linking one's feet from the beach and out across the channel to the far shore. More connected and tugging than the nonchalant hop by air from swinging door to swinging door. With their glimpse of Dover, Marie and Thoby grew restless.

" If we're going back, might as well do it in style, *and*, quietly ! "

Any excuse to go 'down to the sea again' invariably swayed Thoby. With Marie in tow, even the ferry seemed mundane, and so he congratulated himself for having called up his friend and solicitor.

Good old Algie...bachelor and true loner, and more importantly, committed salt. Married to the law, his mistress was the prized '*Rigged Jury*', a sleek, 44' wood-strake ketch. His ritual dash for freedom lay in off-season solo-sailing up and down the Channel and the French-Belgian coast: 'no finer way for an Englishman to become an insurance statistic Thoby…we all become one sooner or later.'

Brilliantly, the call found Algie Pemberton lying barely two kilometers off Le Touquet at the tip of the long bay leading down into Étaples, another stone's throw below Boulogne.

" Thoby ! Good to hear your clarion self ! You had me worried. How fares the 'unreachable source', our dashing champion, elusive as the 'safe' cigarette ? Have I missed another bombshell while out on the bounding main…no, don't tell me, you're being held by agents of *Gitanes* in Mont St. Michel ? – *who-o-ee*, that was a roller ! – still there ? Would've buzzed you some time ago, but must report my chambers phone is bugged, and mobiles are dicey. You remain *very* popular... "

Marie wished that wasn't the case, but smiled supportively.

" …of course, my pleasure absolutely ! Ship of fools, what ? Can bring you up to date on your estate proceeds, lucky fellow, and yours truly can write the voyage off…though *caveat*, Thoby, only one extra suit on-board; best buy some weather gear for your comrade. Can't miss me, pinkish jib always up: deters cocktail invites. Do see if you can filch a good *Chambertin* for the occasion – Thoby, *so glad* to hear there's a companion… cheers lad ! "

Thoby was ebullient.

" What luck Marie, a private 'cruise' back to old Britannia ! And under the command of my confidant, my Little John…and, we'll have to go through Étaples: charming fishing village – now I think of it, wouldn't be surprised if Lilian didn't labour there.

I have this faint recollection it was a medical station of some sort during the First War… ”

Indeed, signs boasted of local herring bakes and festivals as The Thin Man and his shapely partner blew into taples off the train less than three hours later. It almost seemed too much, though fitting, that the taxi taking them to the yacht basin at one point turned down 'Avenue des Canadiens'. Marie nearly missed it, poring over tourist pamphlets from the station.

Thoby's memory was sound: by 1917, the immediate region had supported sixteen hospitals and a convalescent depot; 100,000 allied wounded and reinforcement troops had populated the surrounding dunes. Scores of other Canadians had not chosen, willingly, to stay on in the nearby acres of faithfully tended green fields.

They located the *Chambertin*, and Algie, without a hitch. A tour of all his nifty nautical fittings and a galley which shamed the Ritz kitchens was followed by an on-board Yule feast. Coquilles St. Jacques, lamb loins and Portobello mushrooms, a monstrous green salad, and 'flagons' of wine, consecrated their 'raid' on the continent. For Marie, it also launched a voyage to the New World she now charted. Under the spell of wind, wine, and a fresh future, Marie collapsed dreamily into her bunk and fell asleep attended by the faint cries and whispers of soldiers, patients, and not long afterwards, Lilian…

Tired young feet moved the veteran teenager down rows of pleading cots, sweet smile pinned to her khakis, *'Are you tucked in then…back in just a few days laddie…plump your pillow Major ? …yes of course I'll pass it along to her, but you'll be back in England before it gets there, you'll see...Oh now, Corporal, I'm flattered, but what would your girl say...* "

Algie and Thoby got into the *Remy* and debated the impact and future risk of his tobacco campaign. The solicitous solicitor picked up the torch from Marie and urged the lower road. Feelers out to his shadier contacts had met with firm advice that tobacco killed in more ways than merely sucking on the stuff.

" Marie's true-blue, Thoby, and bang-on about having done your bit. Loads you can still do, no question – and count me in as one of your merry thieves – but why not carry on subversively, more *indirectly*, keep your principles and still draw breath to enjoy this lovely Canuck. Listen chum, *Coke* forgive me, *she's* 'the real thing' – sounds like she loves books, loves the greats, and I want to hear buckets more of her criminal stories. Don't jeopardize that for the sake of open warfare with these weasels...toss the blunt instrument and get more devious; we lawyers are good at that... "

Marie woke fleetingly at the word, 'Yarmouth'. Algie was describing their course to West Wight, rounding the Needles and Alum Bay. She piped up briefly with one directive.

" Perfect, Thoby...seen it on the map...only a short hike over to Freshwater Bay. We are *willed* to pay our respects to Julia and *Dimbola*. Goodnight... "

The Isle of Wight, Île d'Orléans, Mme Bédard pouring tea for Mrs. C....rowing home to haven in sunny...

Nightmares no longer ravaged Thoby's sleep; not since Marie and Switzerland. He felt so braced at the moment, however, vino notwithstanding, that he rejected sleep, determined to take the 'watch', though not sailing till dawn, and commit emotions to paper. The land of his boyhood would rise on the morning horizon. It was right they approached by water…he wanted to record his taking on a fresh pilot – his godsend, out ahead all along – in a metaphor she understood with him. He was amazed at how love loosened a clogged pen…

You could barely see the three of them, ragged denim scalliwags, drifting through the afternoon smaze: Huck, Tom, and their saved confederate, Thoby. The breeze, gossamer-soft, rose and fell soundlessly like a canvas ruffling. The river current was gentle but steady. Only once in a long while did Tom have to nudge the stern pole in the crotch-stick to keep them in the main stream.

The whole raft dipped an inch below the surface when Thoby leapt up suddenly and threw his arms to the sky like a man crucified with joy.

" Tarnation, men ! I feel like someone's left me the full cider jug while the schoolhouse burns to the ground. Why did I never see her before – she was right there in the trees we passed a 1000 times. Her eyes have got me now. It's tolerable fierce but magical… "

The corncob pipe permanently set in Huck's mouth turned upside down, and he cursed the hot ash.

" Men, it's powerful hard to say " Thoby persisted, now he knew his course, " but… "

" Thoby, you ain't fixin' to leave us, " Huck said. " Us pirates is still thick, ain't we " ?

" Naw, that's not it men. But there's sarten shor a corner of the raft for her now. I'm for goin' back – I couldn't never pass another bend knowin' she's back there, lookin' out... "

The confederate looked at Tom pleadingly. Tom had experience with wimmin things, Becky Thatcher an' all. Tom broke down and allowed a smile to rearrange his freckles. The long reed of grass shifted carefully from one side of the mouth to the other before he said, quietly, " He's got the thing bad, Huck... "

Another pause while the shadow of an eagle wafted overhead. Huck challenged, triumphantly, " Would she die for us ? "

Thoby heard himself reply without blinking, " I'd die for her like I'd die for you. "

Huck stared at Tom by way of consultation for some time, then looked Thoby square in the eyes. " It's done then, " he pronounced, " all for one, shor'nuff for ever. "

And then Thoby smiled through his whole body, as together, they worked the raft back upstream apiece, to fetch her.

He hadn't beamed with self-delight in years, if ever. He wedged his masterpiece into the bristles of Marie's hair brush and sat back on his bunk, falling asleep in that position while staring at her beauty.

**

Time held me green and dying
Though I sang in my chains like the sea

Dylan Thomas

Dimbola Lodge, Isle of Wight
December 10, 1917

Joseph Garnet Hébert stared blankly through the tall east windows, over Terrace Lane and the clover sloping down to Freshwater Bay. A sun-burst beat the swell hammering the shore into a radiant turquoise, but the sudden warmth on the sea failed to hearten the 17 year-old Lance Corporal.

Eighteen years earlier, his father had convalesced in England, after the Canadian fling at Paardeberg, then taken a nurse from Surrey home as a trophy to rile the family at Lévis. On this chill afternoon, however, late in an equally futile struggle, the young NCO was oblivious of the environment and his niche in the cycle. And so he'd remained since mid-morning, November 6. Blasted from the teenager's recall was the July dawn when larks and camomile and wormwood had risen magically from the stench and apparitions to quell any last bravado, implanting a simple rage to live.

Joseph's initial survival had been miraculous. When he lurched back against the second wave of his company's advance on Passchendaele, gripping his Sergeant's arm, the stretcher-bearers who finally wrested him from the severed limb and the rabid lashings of an Imperial officer, joked that his body had absorbed so much shell fragment he should have been dumped in the ammo wagon and not the ambulance.

The miracle eluded Joseph, and was duly ignored by the brass. 'Neurasthenia' posed a novel and unpalatable diagnosis, subversive to the cause, and in Joseph's case therefore, as in many others, the General Staff discredited it. Especially after learning of his failed escape bid via Étaples.

There would, consequently, be no intercession by Canadian superiors. No mitigation allowed from the compassionate General Currie, who'd visited the lonely Corporal at his forward O.P. the night before the advance. And thus it mattered not that a willowy creature named Amanda Franklin ministered around the clock to this handsome, startled victim.

In ten days, a squad of twelve men, three of whom he'd personally shielded from machine-gun fire as they slithered from a bombed-out nest at Vimy, would shoot Joseph dead at a stake.

For cowardice in the face of the enemy.

Part V

Crossing the Bar

(17)

October, 1875
Freshwater Bay, I.O.W.

The moon rose from the ocean table to show her own pale silver. A hush of deference blew out of Afton, across Freshwater Bay, then disappeared into the clouds scudding off the great whale's back of the Down.

" There ! *'An' up she rises'*…as radiant as your own true spirit. "

It was a pair cloaked in fond conspiracy that descended from *Dimbola* after a late afternoon tempest into a glittering vesper.

Events had stolen a march on the speaker's habitually cosmic thoughts, and he scrambled to get in step. He paused to measure the unvarnished sincerity, the unassailable truth behind his flattery. " How many flights, I wonder, have we watched her take above our paradise…how many wanderings have *we* made beneath her light, summer and winter, dear lady… "

The male towered in a cape and broad-rimmed hat beside his dour-faced, female companion. He looked veritably Merlin-esque, a diviner of the inner spheres, half-saddened by what he saw, half master of its interpretation. The aura of melancholy which gloomed in his beard, large aquiline features, and sallow, verging-on-dusky complexion, dissolved in laughing, hazel eyes. The woman, superficially unendowed and in no peril of being taken for a naiad on the prowl, appeared equally rapt in affairs of the deeper sort, but was swathed in bright scarves and shawl over skirts stained and reeking with flour and chemicals. Her manner spoke of one who strode full-throttle into life, and from the frequent bending down of the other to engage her response, one perhaps the focus of the occasion.

" Will you abandon us, Julia ? I…I can't ignore the ghosts along the track. I hear a wailing from the legion of souls you've kidnapped and immortalized with that fiendish contraption of yours, myself included – though I admit concealing a grain of essence to keep your painful attentions ! " He waved both arms to encompass the local universe, and his face, had a Victorian novelist been present to describe it, 'implored the heavens'. " How sorely missed in all our haunts…these many years pursuing the gleam…it's been so, so… "

The *mot juste* rarely eluded H.M.'s poet Laureate, but standing now beside his ardent patron at the Albion's seawall, with the elements dancing in a soft breeze, his tongue fell silent, and he retreated into a long pull on his clay pipe.

" …so *noble*, Alfred, so much *beauty* we have chased together, and *found* ! "

" I pray that may be so, Mrs. C…but, you haven't answered. Your fine sons, surely they have the plantations in hand; they're young and sound, and there are such fevers out there. I fear… "

" Our sons *are* there Mr. T., and so therefore my heart, and thus, the *very reason* Charles and I must return…no less than your own treasure lies *here*, amidst the birdsong and the air of *Farringford.* "

It was an inevitable watershed, an unscheduled moment of reflection causing wave upon wave of rich memory to roll over the two icons. The Camerons and Tennysons had hosted unique times at Freshwater. Together they'd spun a 'circle' of inspired characters, from painters and thinkers to parlour maids and village toddlers: Jowett and Darwin; the sculptor and portraitist, G.F Watts; his estranged bride and darling of the world stage, Ellen Terry; the rebel, Garibaldi; Lewis Carroll; their island 'neighbour' and camp-follower, Prince Albert; the poets, Longfellow, Sir Henry Taylor and Robert Browning…

The mournful eyelids brimmed as Tennyson recalled the afternoon, twelve years before, when his dear friend came flying up the path to *Farringford*, flushed and proud, cradling a print of little Annie Philpot, 'my first success'. That day launched a bewildering cavalcade of sitters inveigled into depicting epic themes in history and literature. No one was safe from being dragged into Julia's converted glasshouse studio: innocent wee-tads like Miss Troubridge, the Madonna-incarnate, May Hillier, friends, relations, politicos and poulterers. Some were not dragooned to model anything or anyone, but were subjected, as if in an operating theatre, to letting the camera probe and scrape beneath their brows. With cajoling, some luck, and deliberate disfocusing, the 'terror of Terrace Lane' had exposed the mystique of some of the world's great minds for posterity.

Tennyson had immediately recognized and not shrunk from terming Julia's work as 'art'. It was his view that she had peaked early with a controversial series of images of her niece and Virginia Woolf's mother, Mrs. Herbert Duckworth. More than once he swore to Mrs. C. that their diffuse, transcendant quality would stand as a 'beacon' for the psyche of every later woman. Without resentment, he wondered if her legacy might not outlive that of many of her acclaimed subjects.

Those who ventured into their corner of the Isle were bombarded by the warm vitality of the two households. The Tennyson and Cameron children must have giggled to see imposing adults trail dutifully outdoors after Mrs. Cameron to dance under the stars, or follow her storm-candle onto a windy Down: her's was often a fresh-air salon. Inside *Dimbola*'s panelled halls, one seldom retired early free of Julia's piano or an impassioned recital from the immortal poets, or peals of laughter from guests yielding to assigned roles in impromptu after-dinner sketches.

For the world and for each other.

Alfred's Emily had helped lay out the Camerons' first garden. With typically intransigent purpose, Julia had recently delivered her final plates to illustrate the second volume of the *Idylls*.

It had been a singular passage. As Anny Thackeray afterwards reported, Tennyson's Freshwater era was considered by some as an 'Athens' under Pericles. A Camelot of sorts may well have existed, and Julia, with her passionate loyalty, only enhanced that myth when Alfred thanked her there, under the calm night sky, for her constant labours.

" It is immortality for me to be bound up with you, Alfred. "

He wavered between smiles and tears. He'd often chided the photographer for making his face so notorious that ale cost him double in mainland pubs, but now he was profoundly moved, realizing the impending loss of a kindred spirit. As if anything Julia Margaret Cameron decided ever required affirmation, two wooden coffins already lay on the wharf at Yarmouth beside the luggage, pre-assembled for her and Charles' ultimate destination beyond Ceylon. It left the bard shaken, reminded of one of his own phrases, '*the cold altar of reason*'. He felt oddly vulnerable, restless, frantic even, as he sensed something fundamental falling irretrievably away. It went far beyond poetic introspection…

" What was it all about, what was our searching really *for*… was it all worth it ? Can we have deceived ourselves dear lady? " Tennyson mused on this a little space. " I have the thanks of the 11th Hussars, and certain critics to be sure, and the Queen's blessing at that, but in the greater scheme of things…maybe we were too spoiled, too content on our little foreign strand… "

" *Alfred !* It was our grand and solemn duty, the embodiment of my prayers that we should encounter and record so much human grandeur…all that we could see, feel, touch…? And mercy ! You have only to think of Lionel, Hallam, and yourself, towed by kites along the crest. Such joy, such proximity in every way to the ether… "

At that instant, Tennyson saw the countenance of this dowdiest plain-Jane of seven sisters in a wholly new light.

Her's is a lovely face; God has indeed lent her much in saving grace...and he took comfort.

" I stand rebuked...the flowers planted, trees tended, fruits harvested, all the thrilling weather diarized with the trail of so many fine and varied visitors. I think on it Julia; you may physically sail away, but I cannot imagine that our spirits will not both remain to care for this place – that said, I find myself drained of the right words... "

" Oh Alfred, forgive me, but you've already said them: '*may there be no sadness of farewell, when I embark...*'

So he had. The sheer magnificence of the evening and the immensity of the parting at hand now overwhelmed him, and Alfred Tennyson was in fact speechless.

He looked over the wall at the glistening stones which caught his gaze; they seemed to chase after the running tide, and he had to move. He patted Julia's shoulder and went down the few steps to the beach. The poet stooped, and felt the dolorous weight of his laurel tumble into the foam. He selected a perfectly round flat stone, brushing off any speck of sand, lest it alter the intended course.

Then, in miraculous restoration of his youth, he swung his arm forward at waist-level, flicking his wrist effortlessly to launch the disc. It skipped bravely five or six times, wobbled, then tagged a ripple and sank. Tennyson's brow rose and fell with the fortunes of the stone.

He couldn't bear the obvious metaphor.

(18)

He rose at dawn, fired with hope,
Shot o'er the seething harbour bar,
And reached the ship and caught the rope,
And whistled to the morning star

Tennyson

the English Channel
Wednesday, December 21

The spume was ice-cold and stung. It felt superb on her cheeks as Marie braced herself at a wild angle beside Algie in the stern cockpit, enthralled by the borderless world of craft and sea. Thoby was forward, leaning both forearms on the rail above the bowsprit, nosing into the moment like a little boy, happily drenched in his weather gear. She felt like an affirmative-action pirate, fleeing a raid on the French coast, with her male booty safely stowed under a salty eye.

Algie had them up and coffee'd – 'cognac no object, maties' – by 4:00 a.m., a godly or ungodly hour, depending how religious one's sea fever; but now the brilliant day was unequivocally spiritual in its noiseless rhythm.

The three chalk stacks of the '*Needles*' continued growing off the starboard. Marie admired the dramatic 40-meter wedges, mutually isolated but all pressing back against the long down defining the west end of Wight. Algie had been tracking the great stone cross raised for Tennyson at roughly the mid and highest point of the down for the last hour. Marie knew it viscerally as something special, a 'sign' in the classic sense: a lighthouse, a beckoning tree meant to be seen by her then, and precisely then.

" Whole tip's a geographic gem apparently, coloured sand, oodles of nifty mineral strata…which is actually all I know about it Marie. But *hey* ! Did you know Marconi set up a station right there ? Sent his first transmission to channel-boats pretty well where we're cutting through now…blew Queen Vickie away by radioing the royal house at Osborne. "

Within minutes, they'd rounded the *Needles* to enter the Solent and Alum Bay, bearing for Yarmouth, with the Dorset coast running along the port.

Thoby hadn't spoken for ages; the moisture in Marie's eyes when she read his Mark Twain conceit that morning had clinched his heart irrevocably. There *was* going to be a second chance, a fresh start, and he lost himself to introspection. *I've been a shell my whole life*…and he only understood that now he learned what it was to feel complete. Staring beneath his feet, midmorning, at the bow bisecting the foam, he met with a day-version of the 'Vienna' dream which had marked his earlier ferry crossing. This time, when the man moved to the side of the bridge where the blue turbulence of history rushed out, it wasn't as a solitary figure; there was a woman too, with her arm around his waist. Thoby didn't need to see her face.

It was just after noon when Thoby worked his way aft and the gentle sweep of Totland Bay succeeded the craggy swirl of Alum.

" Well my little ambulance driver, all ready ? "

It was Marie's spur of the moment idea, and Algie was so accommodating. No need to go all the way to Yarmouth; they could leave non-essentials with him, take his large back-pack, and jump ship below Totland proper. Algie said there was a splendid pier there in fact, no need to row in with 'muffled oars'. They could grab tea somewhere, and still have time for a healthy ramble up to the Cross, then push on down to the Albion Hotel at Freshwater Bay. The *Rigged Jury*'s ship-to-shore would gladly book a room under the name of 'Mr. & Mrs. Locksley'. Algie had grinned, " We are, after all, a 'full-service' firm… "

Any incidental confusion for the dark side would be a bonus...

Marie and Thoby turned and waved from the last of the wood steps which carried their drunken sea-legs to the cliff-top. Far out below, Algie's pink jib fluttered goodbye from a choppy, sparkling Solent. They turned again and padded a hundred yards across a park bordering the cliff, laughing at their gait. They were greeted at the other edge by a brick Victorian mansion, with ornate grounds and scads of windows fronting the ocean. The '*Sentry Mead*' guest house drew them in without a murmur of protest.

After sherry, a mound of scones – Marie graciously 'slumming' with raspberry jam in lieu of blackcurrant – and two pots of Earl Grey, they were off again, with promises to stay another time, and directions out of Totland up to the Down. The weather held cool and clear; for Marie, much like a brilliant Quebec autumn afternoon.

They found the village cenotaph standing at the end of the *Sentry*'s street in the hub of diverging roads. Even more attuned since their first encounter, Marie and Thoby scanned the names of those killed in the Second War, touched for their effort by seeing three local boys had perished in the Canadian merchant navy and the Canadian army engineers.

They bore left after the monument, as directed, immediately congratulating themselves for hoofing it. The country-side, which inundated everything rather than be crushed by box and concrete, sloped steadily up to the right, fields edged with woods, mint-scented paths canopied by soft leafy elms and chestnuts linking the two. A castle turret poked above a treed gully to the left and east, stately manors and thatched cottages were splotched here and there, all painted into a nestled time-warp. And the cross. Tennyson's Cross was visible almost from the outset, ahead and off to the right, a sure guide by land or sea.

" Thoby, 'beautiful' hardly begins – *c'est le vrai de vrai.* " She paused comfortably to gather the key elements of her jury summation. " I've found more serenity, more insight on my sorry self in sailing from France and our first two hours on land than a glob of shrinks could ever bleed from me. I look around, breathe this air, and forget I used to spend ninety per cent of my time pleading the fraudulent, unsound causes of second-rate people, and a hundred per cent of it suppressing instinct and desires…forgot what simple independence was. I don't feel the need to defend myself, pursuing Julia Cameron. A journey into the 'past' is an enriching thing – *say it's so* Thoby; I mean, that's *my* chosen reality, *my life* as I sure as hell intend to live it... "

Thoby looked tenderly at this proclamation bound in loose khakis, turtleneck, and a periwinkle bandana highlighting smooth, dusky skin, the more lush with the rose of exercise. Her sudden rant ended with a scornful swipe.

" …I need innocence, a shot of eccentric legend – yes, I know, 'I *vant* to be alone'! A dash of old-fashioned gentility against an age of 'in your face'. Reassurance that beauty may survive the strip mall and homogenized culture… "

" Wow, great lecture kiddo ! You shouldn't be allowed too much ocean air…Seriously though, how can a poor sod seeking the once-noble gang of his youth do ought but crumple at your brave feet in total, abject fealty ? "

Thoby let slip the backpack and lay prostrate, cupping both Marie's ankles in his hands, entreating the laneway. " Now sweet voyager, now, let loose your birds of joy, let them flock to our several quests and sail above us ever… "

Marie, who'd already stunned herself by pledging to this reformed mercenary, shrieked with laughter, and cheered the gods for pricking it. She leaned over and pulled him up playfully by both ears until he met her eyes, then kissed him hard on the mouth.

" Everything here pulls me, some demonic stimulus, everything *resonates*… "

" You do look the pilgrim, dear heart…*mercy* ! "

After that, they hit a pleasant stride. One of the gratuitous attributes to leak from the re-work in progress known as Thoby Carlyle, was the welcome fact he was a maniacal footballer – not the *couch* or *drink yourself blotto* sub-species, but an honest-to-god player. The kind that dribbles anything remotely round, inside *or* outside, then drops dead on the pitch at eighty, executing the perfect header. He had legs of steel, and Marie loved them for both reasons.

A small church terminated the upward road at what appeared about a third of the way towards the cross, so they swung left on a lovely lane, a road clearly less traveled. Fifty yards or so in, Marie called a halt; she was almost dizzy with exuberance, and wanted a moment just to savour the adventure, take stock of their day.

They lay back, still standing, against a high grassy bank. They both gazed up and day-dreamed for awhile, until Marie broke the natural silence.

" It's *December* Thoby, and look: wild roses, bramble flowers, and *real holly* ! We're in Neverland… "

Indeed, the whole scape of child-like counterpane exuded a deep composure. History seeped from every green pore: Roman, piratical, literary, and just plain pastoral. One could rely on it staying there, as is, constant through storm *und drang.* Even the infamous Isle of Wight Rock festival and the Rolling Stones could only add colour and fail to shake the sacred continuity. So English, so off-shore. Marie slipped into a congenial trance.

She saw herself and Thoby *ad idem* on the legitimate motive for inward treks. She was confident she'd brought Thoby round to where he no longer felt tyrannized by the past, only impelled by or archaeological about it, going behind it, picking about for icons and heroes to rekindle. Now he could shun tobacco and vanish into the leaves of Sherwood, and she…well, admittedly 'born' in the nineteenth century, could revisit the epistles of that era's stellar women, learn how to nurture what mattered to *her*. Marie's soul rushed all over this new Île d'Orléans, then came to rest, eyes wide open…

" Thoby, I've…Thoby ? "

" *Ta-da-da-dat-da-dah* ! Behind you fair maiden, and that's a bugle in case you wondered, *summoning* you ! Got shivers all over, and so will you when you see this, come on… "

Out of sheer curiosity, Thoby had hopped the rise behind and gone into the grove only ten yards before discovering a tiny graveyard. In one corner, a solid white cross set in crushed stone distinguished itself dramatically from the other grey, collapsing slabs. Stark black letters etched in the white marker read simply:

Alfred Noyes
Poet
1880 – 1958

" Here's the man himself, Marie ! The pied piper back to the proverbial halls of my youth…wrote *Sherwood*. Can you believe it, just resting right here in…in Tennyson's shadow for Pete's sake ! Neighbours and kindred spirits – *The Highwayman* ! And we just happened by. What say we thunder by tonight on horses and hurl a blood-red rose at his feet ? "

" Sounds *romantic* Thobs, but forgive your lover if she hasn't read that one… "

" No fear damsel, but don't let anyone at the hotel point anything lethal at those breasts tonight, especially if wearing a red coat… " And he swept his willing captain into an Errol Flynn embrace. " D'you know he did intelligence with John Buchan in the First War, spent most of the Second in Canada… so damn nifty to come upon him today of all days. He always said the only thing that mattered was chasing the sound of 'happy children's feet' – well Mr. Noyes, sir, I *hear* you, and Robin Hood's *awake* ! " Thoby leapt from the rise back to the lane, sword at the ready.

They agreed they'd been officially welcomed.

Emerging from the 'forest', Thoby traveled even lighter. Any vestige of gross ambition and personal suffering had fallen finally away; only a sudden vigour seized him. There'd been a demi-life in that little wood: half perhaps the spiritual energy emitted by the interred, half the projection of the Quick's desire for continuity. And *he*'d answered.

Marie was impressed by the unheralded interlude. No hot-dog stands and signs promising orgasmic family fun for miles beforehand, with a theme park at the end. Back in London, when she shared her devotion to the well-spring of arts and letters once trickling between *Farringford* and *Dimbola*, Marita remarked that few in England were aware of Freshwater, let alone its thriving Victorian 'circle', or for that matter, Wight itself, beyond some day-tripper come-ons at Ryde on the Portsmouth side.

Yes, there would surely be many such surprises here, lots of hidden corners, poignant rewards waiting for the open heart…

**

" Jesus bloody Christ in the bloody morning, *Neale* ! "

A phone call to his London flat from Prinsep forced Neale to admit he had no current dope on the target.

He'd exhausted every contact on his mobile. They hadn't taken the Calais ferry, not yet anyway…what if they didn't come back at all ? *Shit* ! Neale couldn't accept that he'd misjudged the pair. For one not burdened with intellect or moral balance, his trajectories on human behaviour usually met with vindication.

Even so, Prinsep had once chewed him out in front of the Vice-Chair, the only exec at B.A. for whom he'd ever been trotted out face-to-face. What hurt was that it followed a botched arson – child disfigured, the parent unscathed – which nevertheless achieved the desired silence.

'*Neale here, is like a knife without a blade, for which the handle is missing,*' Prinsep had sneered.

He hated the man, and now Neale's lazy assumption might hand him a bat to knock the props out from his recent 'leaves on the track' illusion.

His reputation was at stake; or rather, *self-respect*, as Neale's professional credits didn't lend themselves to public accolade. Only two discernible 'goals' sat on an uncluttered horizon: screw Prinsep and B.A. for good, after dazzling execution of a key contract; and, taking possession of this hypnotic 'Marie'. He cared more about the woman than the primary hit, but understood the one fed the other.

" Neale, it is *imperative* that Carlyle be removed from our list of liabilities *this week…* "

The fresh verbal dictate issued Wednesday afternoon.

When one's world rests on shifting sand, however, immediate pleasures oft prevail. And so while his master barked, Neale could only picture the statuesque diva of divas who was billed to sing for the lucky few two days hence on the I.O.W. With that vision dangled in front of his rheumy eyes, all goals and desires – the two he had – tended to scatter like pigeons in Trafalgar when the guns roar salute.

" …after Friday, there will be an issue of diminishing returns for your retainer, and for yourself at B.A. – get the blessed job done man ! The only call I want from you is friggin' confirmation… "

**

Love took up the harp of life,
and smote all the chords with might;
Smote the chord of Self, that, trembling,
pass'd in music out of sight

Tennyson

" Oh Thoby, it's breathtaking ! No roof on your thoughts... "

Lime-green carpet ran from where they emerged from the gorse on the backside of Tennyson's Cross, to the knee-weakening drop, ten yards beyond, into the chalk-blue paste of sky and sea. Out where they'd sailed *their* toy boat only that morning.

It was while cavorting about the crown, a 360° window on Wight, the Solent and the Channel – mussing their hair and looking dramatically mournful, Heathcliff imploring Catherine – that Marie first appreciated the region's light. A special quality, an unhindered clarity which had the effect, she realized, of cleansing both sight and perception, letting one see the true milieu. Marie speculated how Julia must have divined the value of shadow, of lightness and darkness simply because of the pure, ambient luminosity. The fervent heart, the depth of loss and nobility, the essence within, were captured by playing with degrees of light, shunning formality for animus revealed.

One thing for sure, Marie was 'home'. By the time they left, the giant cross had become a 'friend', nothing melancholy at all, more of a looming shepherd who offered calm. An anchor holding down a safe harbour.

" Thoby, I can't wait, we're so near. We'll be up here a million times, let's go down to *Dimbola* now….already 'gone half four' as you would say. We can cut off to the left here and save time... "

Marie had stumbled into her first marriage almost negligently and it had eroded with an appropriately blasé tristesse. She was more nervous now as a sincere novitiate, closing in on more faithful ground.

They half-picked, half- pitched their way down a large rut trailing off at a right angle from the ridge through several lines of shrub, trees, and as the terrain leveled, a cow's gate, through which they sidled, expectant as children on a lark. A treed path led them two or three hundred meters between a pig farm and a clover field and deposited them ultimately at the same fork, and the very same Orchard Bros. shop which Charlotte had patronized eighty-one years before.

The daylight now burnished all it still reached; a pink-gilt bathed the thatch on St. Agnes, a quaint stone church backing on a meadow along to their right.

Marie tugged Thoby's arm. " *That* way – *Farringford* tomorrow. "

Marie as tour guide. It wasn't instinct so much as she realized she'd always belonged here, might truly live here, where her heart – and that was the instinct part– naturally resided. Whatever romantic, valued, spiritual 'thing' would form her life-marker, would stand here, and it would be her own, because *she*'d let herself be drawn and would, she was absolutely certain, choose to stay. From the dark and cherished corridor of her first encounters, tumbled the thrill of classic tales, treasured scenes, deathless words and inspirational figures with all their imagined touchstones, morphing now into the sights and sounds of Wight.

She recalled churning out her senior thesis, sparked by the iconoclasm of highborn Victorians like Cameron and Nightingale. In an age when life expectancy rejoiced in 65, they spent passion, brains, and good old indomitable will to preserve the bodies and souls of their world. By sheer commitment, and with no brooch of 'feminism' pinned to their breast, they managed to exalt humanity while challenging the female stereotype.

Only, Marie had 'betrayed' that legacy – or so she coloured her descent into the male caverns of law and politics, spurning finer beauty for clever mind-games – and it was that gradual discovery and self-contempt which rallied her eventual retreat from the plains of Quebec. Now here she was, mere steps from her patient Mecca ! She planted herself at the curb, one arm on her hip, the other outstretched, as if pointing out something plainly visible.

" Can you *see* them, the two of them, arm in arm, coming down the way. Laughing at some rhyme of Edward Lear's, plotting skits for after dinner, conspiring to place Longfellow beside Dodgson at supper ? My God, Thobs ! Life before the blue flickering screen and talk-shows and drive-throughs – promise me we'll walk *every* night, and talk and recite, *ohh…* "

After St. Agnes, the road bent and dipped towards the bay. From their approach, Marie and Thoby saw a great tree on the left arching over the crest, and on the opposite side, a two-storey beige structure with a large bay window hanging out as if to share the ocean view at the far end. Below the window, a sign pointing in towards the building read 'Terrace Lane'.

Marie expected the doyenne to bustle out to greet them, or shoe them into the converted chicken coop for an extended sitting.

Turning in, they found the immediate corner of the first level adapted into a rare and used books shop. The rest of the structure ran back along the lane in a fine jumble of large rectangular windows and bays which posed minimal interference with a spectacular seaward prospect. A square turret anchored the central façade, with two storeys of windows above the tall doors at the bottom. The latter opened into a front hall, with a broad staircase turning up at the back, a lovely, cloth-tabled tea-room off to the left, and an elderly woman with a brusque eye surveying Thoby and Marie from a desk behind the door to the right.

" We're closing actually… " But that was as far as she got in raising the nightly drawbridge; the look in Marie's eyes stayed her hand. " but if you'd care for a quick look-round, it's not been what you'd call a hectic day, and there is some *exquisite* fresh carrot cake would go to waste without attention… "

" That's extremely kind of you – be back tomorrow in 'full force', but we've come *so far* today, a quick peek would be fabulous… "

“ Splendid. You take that peek and I’ll have Fiona get some tea going. ”

Marie felt a peculiar twinge, as if she were herself a member of the household. She pictured ‘Fiona’ fleeing at the mention of her name to avoid insertion in some bizarre tableau for the mistress’ camera.

Toby paused to enjoy the feel of the entrance and its dark wood paneling. The lady minding the door chimed in with how Mrs. Cameron had added the faux Gothic tower to unite the two original halves of the structure, thus creating *Dimbola Lodge*.

His gaze moved down the wide stairwell along the walls, until it was arrested by the brooding, soul-searching eyes of a woman of classical features.

“ ‘Mrs. Herbert Duckworth’, Mrs. Cameron’s niece. Quite powerful… ” chimed the lady once more, and she had good reason to be of such opinion, having done battle with the countenance daily for some years. “ …taken in 1865. ”

Thoby shook his head slowly. Nearly a century and a half later, it compelled verbal response. It dawned on him he’d seen the same face on an old post-card clipped inside Marie’s diary. Given his own perdition, and now inexplicable – touch wood – Second Chance, the near-rapturous melancholy seized his heart.

When he turned around, Marie had disappeared.

“ She’s gone up, ” said the lady-in-waiting.

Thoby smiled. *Vanished, like a spirit to the source…*

He found her on the second floor, silhouetted against the large bay window they'd seen from the lane, in an unheated chamber strewn with books and papers. A glass vase filled with fresh delphiniums stood on the ledge looking down to the ocean.

The view, and the intoxicating scent, held Marie immobile; Thoby remained equally still, watching her enchantment. Her body eased and she pressed close to the panes, peering both ways up and down, humming abstractedly, vaguely conscious she was scanning below for guests or notable passers-by.

" Ha ! This room *is* inhabited, decidedly alive… " a voice chuckled from a rear corner.

Both Marie and Thoby started. A pleasant, academic type sat happily ensconced on the floor, sifting through a drawer of documents.

" 'Julian Hynchcliffe', Curator. Often find myself drifting up here too, chatting merrily away with thin air… " His brow furrowed, " thought we'd closed shop for the day, " but the minor formality evapourated instantly. " Speaking of 'alive', the BBC was here last year, doing a docu on the Freshwater Circle – don't suppose you saw it ? No matter, the crew was all on about this awful stink filling the air whenever they came up here. Julia's room you see… "

Marie wasn't surprised.

" …only died off when they packed up. I could never distinctly make it out, but maybe that's because I'm part of the woodwork. Their description of the odour boggles the mind though, totally consistent with the chemicals she used in her developing process – got that verified by a scientist chap. Stuff apparently soaked into her clothes and hands all the time. In fact, some swear it killed her prematurely…*anyway*, Fiona puts flowers up here in case it's just a dead mouse behind the baseboards. "

" Not fair, " said Marie reflexively, " when it was part of something creative… "

" American are you ? ", now he heard one of them speak.

" No-o-o. " For once, Marie didn't mind. " disciple from Canada. "

" And her local partner in crime, " beamed Thoby.

" Photographers on a pilgrimage...? "

Marie was aware of an intense stillness in the room. One or two after-beams played on the ledge through the vase. She remembered later how all three of their faces were tilted in a soft focus amid the deepening shadow, there being no electric lights in the room. Whatever was beautiful about the moment was frozen in an eternal frame.

" No, " answered Marie. " I can't lay claim to an artistic calling… " Then she laughed, gesturing at Toby, " except for retouching this Cambridge relic, I'm… " She paused and looked suddenly up at the ceiling, adding wistfully, " not an angel of charity like my nineteenth century sisters… " In her own universe, she was bowing specifically to Flo and Julia. But the Freshwater drug was taking hold. Already she felt kindred, caring – *human*. *For Christ's sake, that's what it's all about*, *being passionate for what moves you.* The nearer she got to this site of early yearnings, the stronger the pull: the whole journey from Quebec had been following a thread out of Minos.

" Well… " Hynchcliffe read her silence; Thoby was caught off-guard by the slide into the pensive by his usually flamboyant mate. " at least you're reflecting where she so often did – '*Cambridge*' did you say ? When? What was your… "

" Chemistry, microbiology, " confessed Thoby, as if recalling the Middle Ages.

The curator stared over his readers.

" You look rather my vintage, if you don't mind the slight… possibly have haunted the Poets' Society ? "

Thoby had indeed, briefly. " Made a perfect prat of myself at one sherry affair…not so-brilliant paper on Housman and Noyes… "

Hynchcliffe wobbled to his feet, thrusting out his hand, a smile tearing through a field of age freckles. " '*Sherwood and Shropshire: Where are the Lads ?*' Right ? Stuck with me. Must have been one of the stalwart band, what ! "

Thoby did a double-take, but glowed with the unexpected recognition. Kudos for something untainted in his life, recollected without Marie's encouragement. His cup positively frothed over. " They're doing tea for us downstairs; *do* join us ? Marie will have a thousand questions… "

Marie glided down the staircase behind the two men in a congenial haze, caressing the wood banister, feeling quite proprietarial. At the door to the tea-room – the former front parlour as Hynchcliffe pointed out – a wall photo, as with Thoby, demanded her attention. In it, three army nurses stood behind five young men, all seated and staring out blankly like a group of Stan Laurels. There was a caption on the yellowed matting: '*Canadian convalescents with their guardian 'Blue Birds', Dimbola Lodge, December, 1917'*. The boy on the extreme right, and you couldn't have called him anything else, drew Marie's eye; his face looked away from the camera, well into the distance. It was the absolute image of her maternal grandfather; though maybe the uniform coloured her intuition, and of course, it couldn't have been her grandfather.

Tea was wonderful, and Marie did have a 1000 questions, but her companions were lost momentarily in Cambridge vignette. She left the table several times, busily inspecting the 'sacred precinct', looking about in every direction, trying to recapture and live every view and vestige engaged by the original inhabitants. Then she noticed a stout, obviously antique piano at the other end of the room.

" That was Julia's, " cautioned the curator dutifully, seeing Marie get up and make a bee-line. There were creamers, a china dinner bell, and all manner of Victorian bric-a-brac set along the lid to discourage access to the keys. " It only gets played on very special occasions... "

" Oh... " completely undeterred, " d'you think I might just...? I'd treat it lovingly, " edging closer.

Many had begged before in vain, but this was Marie's day. Her eyes shone as she proceeded to remove all obstructing items and lift the lid with reverence. Hynchcliffe prayed; Thoby was bemused. *Surely not 'chopsticks'*…

Marie glanced out the windows, took two long breaths, then let her fingers hover over the ivory which she who'd tamed Watts, Carlyle, Taylor and Darwin, and so many giants of the intellectual empire, had often touched. The notes floated up by themselves, emotional in their runs, as if already alive without being selected. There was soul and compassion in their release, and Marie began to cry spontaneously as she played. Fiona, the woman at the door, the two college cronies, all were transfixed. They continued silent after Marie finished the piece, one she hadn't even thought about before it came.

" God almighty, that was beautiful… " Hynchcliffe whispered at length. " Liszt ? "

The composer's name hung for a second in the after-notes.

" *Liebestraum* " smiled Marie, emerging from her musical séance.

" You never mentioned you played… " stammered Thoby, rushing over proudly to hug the pianist from behind.

" I blush for having hesitated, " enthused Hynchcliffe. " Jenny Lind sang here for Tennyson, you know – no relation are you ! Julia would be thrilled I have no doubt; I can see her now, scurrying over to line you up for the soiree on the lawn… " But he had the very reward, a veritable bouquet for the performer. " I've two passes left for tomorrow evening – did you know about it perhaps ? "

They didn't.

" The current 'Swedish nightingale', Anne Sofie von Otter, is doing a solo thing at *Farringford* tomorrow – we're a sponsor, but the poet's place has a bigger hall – it's one of our 'thank-you' efforts for patrons and members of the Cameron Trust. Special performance, all her own choice…should be a real treat. By invite only, and *you* belong there ! What do you say ? "

" Oh yes ! We'd love to, wouldn't we Thoby. "

Though sufficiently with-it to recognize the great soprano's name and general stature, sadly, the threat of operatic trills and stentorian leakage drove Thoby to Victor Borge spoofs, allusions to the 'messy soprano' singing 'areas' (because of her inflated size), and the climax 'where she tries to escape the rain barrel and yells for help'.

" Don't think me a cretin, beloved, but sopranos and arias for some lamentable reason grate me like fingernails down a chalkboard – don't know why, maybe my mother dragged me in itchy shorts to one too many recitals – and small salon-type gatherings bring on a wild claustrophobia. Your playing just now was nothing short of magical, and I love the lyrical composers, but… "

" But you'll *come…* "

What was he thinking ! " Of course, my dear Mrs. Cameron, the evening will not fail for my absence – but please don't give me the heave-ho if I slip off to the Down at some point for some wide-open – I promise not to leap… "

" Then you'd miss the champagne, " said Hynchliffe wisely. " You won't regret it, hottest ticket item here this season. In fact, some dark little character, a real *grockle*, came round only this morning, pleading for a poster of the event. "

" 'Grockle' ? " Marie bit. The curator coveted the word; using it made him feel indigenous.

" Local term for off-island people… "

They were out on the pub terrace in no time after checking into the *Albion*, turtlenecked and nursing pints of 'Pirates Brew', watching the tide creep in. The sharpening chill meant nothing to two 'hardy salts' who couldn't let go of the day. Lamb and sticky toffee pudding eventually felled them, but not before a final taste of the sea from their balcony.

Tiny lights darted back and forth around the bay like giant fireflies in the night, with pin-prick sparks stationary behind them. It took a while until Thoby divined they were the tips of the long graceful rods of night anglers. There were at least nine of them they could make out along the seawall, cigarettes flaring in the dark, bundled in vests and parkas, with whisky bottles propped handily at their feet – *tonight's* recital thought Marie...

Thoby faded suddenly, victim of unaccustomed peace. He kissed Marie on the ear and whispered, " Take care in the 'torrent of darkness', " and went in. Marie lingered outside. The cold air only made the waiting duvet more delicious.

Alone, she felt free to romanticize…the fishers were the native chorus, signalers of the rhythm and ritual of the place. Various players stepped from the shadows of the wild and beautiful environment. Marie made a point of greeting them, saluting their passage before her, then bidding goodnight. She had to do that or she'd never sleep; she was conscious of a rising well of energy, long suppressed in logging billable hours and chasing the baubles of 'career'.

A pleasant wreath of tobacco smoke floated up from the men on the seawall.

Marie pondered whether Browning and Taylor had once hurled iambics across the Camerons' table, grabbed their pipes and strode down to the bay to canvass the verdict of the elements. Had Alice Liddell and Anny Thackeray ever become fast friends and shared impressions of that peculiar Oxonian, the Reverend Mr. Dodgson ? And goodness, was that George du Maurier wedged in the rocks below, dashing off a night sketch to impress his fellow guest, G.F. Watts, 'England's Michelangelo' ? And the birds haunting the trees behind the hotel, singing warm-up for Jenny and Anne…the circle, the values surviving. How naturally Marie subscribed. It was black magic !

She wrapped herself in the light and darkness, the salt wisps and pure air, and turned slowly, taking in the stars and remembering the Embankment in London. She was learning the catechism so lovingly scripted by Julia: the sentiment of family, the heart, mind, history and myth – true beauty – everything she found largely absent from the popular easel of the world.

By the time she went into bed, Marie had determined to 'stay on'. They would open a B&B, as the gracious hosts, 'Alfred and Lilian Cameron: *where the old world meets the new'*. She liked that, and no one would ever trace them until a time when no one would any longer care...

Thoby was curled up with the sliding door to the balcony wide open, blissfully plying some wine-dark sea. Crumpled in his bedside basket was a letter Algie had slipped him the night before. It was addressed to Algie on the letterhead of *Champneys Ermengard Dalrymple Clogstoun & Clitheroe, Solicitors*. The writer, who bore none of the latter monikers, begged to have conveyed to Dr. Carlyle, wherever he might be, the profound shock and discomfort his client, British Andorra Tobacco, had suffered by reason of the said Carlyle's continued and unwarranted attacks in the media. The author had had no recourse but to advise his client that Thoby's conduct constituted 'a serious violation of company guidelines as well as a breach of contract'; as a consequence, of course, the said malefactor's pension had been automatically forfeited. Legal action was contemplated for malicious defamation…

Thoby turned in his sleep. One arm clung to a forestay, the other brandished a cutlass. They couldn't know where he was, not in his new happiness. It had to be counter-bluff. If some emissary of corporate goodwill did materialize, he'd kill him, shiver his timbers stem to gudgeon…

(19)

the *Conrad*, Chelsea Harbour, London
December 22

Anne Sofie von Otter was a risk-taker, a diva non-conforming, and her legion of fans adored her. She thrived on innovation and solo recitals as much as she enjoyed conquering Munich, the Met, La Scala, or Covent Garden. Statuesque, with razored blond hair, her wicked eyes flicked from comic to tragic lyricism in the blink of a boundless range.

There wasn't much of value the 'Baroque bombshell' hadn't tried on for size in expanding her repertoire, having worn, triumphantly, the 'trousers' roles for sopranos in *Cherubino*, *Hansel*, and *Orpheus* – and to highlight the intimate solo gig on the Isle of Wight, ending her U.K. swing, von Otter had chosen a personal conceit, and typically, a real challenge. How often had she wept as the great tenors rode Puccini's swelling aria, *Nessun Dorma*, to its groin-rattling peak: why not her ? Couldn't a female voice trigger the same flood of emotion ? The idea struck von Otter as somehow festive, her own decoration on the Yule tree. There was no trepidation on her part whatsoever that it might fall and shatter.

As for the venue, *Farringford*, it looked picturesque, dramatic, set on a long slope down to the ocean. More to the point, it had sheltered her favourite poet, English or otherwise, and as her agent kept mentioning, its same parlour once welcomed her fellow Swede, Jenny Lind, long ago. 'The circle come round Sofie…has a nice cachet.'

" Remember when you sang *Ramiro* in Aix-en-Provence and the guy tore off his tux and shirt and leapt up on the conductor's shell to 'win' your heart ? "

" Ya-a-a. He slipped and broke both legs – but he *was* very handsome… "

" You know what I'm getting at Sofie, " her trusted pianist continued. " If someone can get that close in a major site, imagine an elbow-knocking room like this *Farringfjord*. I worry sometimes… "

" Oh Bengt, I love you for caring, but just make sure there's buckets of egg-nog ! If there's egg-nog, I'll do Schubert or some Mahler just for you ! "

Von Otter waved her sheet music briskly.

" Isn't it inspired ? The unknown prince, ready to die if the cruel but gorgeous Turandot can learn his name before dawn – hey ! the Nordic ice-queen, that's me – but he won't *really* die; it's poetic, romantic to the extreme. He's *smitten* fatally. *Love conquers all* ! "

" You don't sound that glacial… "

" *I'm* the prince, Bengt…at daybreak, *vincerò*, *VINCERÒ !* "

**

Portsmouth
Thursday, December 22

" It's blackmail, cheeky intrusion in our affairs…they're *scum* for Christ's sake ! "

Patrick Sutcliffe, OBE – the harried CFO – and five CEC colleagues dragged back from seasonal excess, were not happy campers this noontide. And it wasn't because they were in any doubt about receiving obscene Christmas bonuses; it was more that visions of Thoby Carlyle ran through their starry-chambered heads. It seemed the elusive scientist was now operating as an equal-opportunity blower.

" And after we sullied ourselves… " Jonathan Silver, Parallel Markets Director, blithely observed.

British Andorra had weathered the recent UDA 'Irish collaboration' smear in the *Times*, thanks in part to a spate of hostage crises in Kabul. Happily, a B.A. scout had been one of the victims, garnering public sympathy for his plight as a Brit businessman cruelly caught in a foreign maelstrom – even though his mission, *Project Khyber*, was to make B.A. brands the number one cause of death in Afghanistan after warlord pogroms.

But now a late-morning thunderbolt had struck, a secure message from '*Claddagh*', the fanatic breakaway wing in County Tyrone. At least two on the Committee were previously ignorant of the firm's unchronicled profit from the 'troubles', but they chose wisely to say nary a word. The latest threat originated in the mid 90's, when B.A. played no favourites, and had trucked with parties other than the UDA in smuggling and money-laundering.

A single hard copy was shared round the table:

Omagh

We have received a demand from one of your own.

Dr. T. Carlyle requires:

- *an immediate press release disassociating our movement from and disavowing contraband tobacco traffic*
- *we pay £3 million immediately – and publicize the fact – in support of lung cancer research in Northern Ireland*
- *fund the creation of a children's fresh-air summer camp outside Londonderry*

Failing compliance with the above:

- *world media will be informed of our past affiliation and joint ventures with yourself*
- *such information would be name and position-specific regarding both parties*
- *any interference with Carlyle's person will automatically activate an untraceable procedure resulting in global distribution of the above information*

The demands must be met and publicly set in motion by Dec. 25.

Our position is that neither of us has plausible impunity in the circumstances. Given time constraints and consequences imposed, punishment action is not considered feasible.

Reply with proposed response and significant financial participation, ASAP.

W. Tone

Not a creature stirred, not even the CFO. All present knew the real impact was on Sir Geoffrey's fortunes, and no one was about to play the Greek messenger. They fooled with their pencils and tried to avoid the many shades of frustration and twitching facial nerves racking the Chairman.

It was notorious that he was in line for the Spanish ambassadorship, the crown on a long public career. The last thing he needed was a scandal surfacing from his watch involving terrorists. Where would his credentials be on sensitive Basque or Catalan issues ? For a purely selfish instant, he threw corporate independence to the wind and mulled drastic action: calling in MI5 markers for B.A.'s cooperation on *Project Kayak* in Dubai, tracing tobacco smuggling money running into Iran for weapons…but he saw it would show a weak hand in dealing with a mere individual, and if every knowledgeable body in the rogue Irish cell weren't silenced, damage could still be done. There was no room to indulge the fond wish that despite *Claddagh*'s formal assessment, some baddies weren't at that minute stocking Carlyle and might snuff the crisis outright. In any event, the Irish wouldn't have contacted B.A. if they weren't feeling vulnerable – not that he cared – so the demand must be serious. O'Leary and Argue were both incumbents enjoying tenuous legitimacy in the coalition government, and could not afford the embarrassment.

It was a bitter, expensive bullet Sir Geoffrey now chose to bite.

" Patrick, leave *now*, contact Prinsep – don't care where he is or if he's at death's door – have him intercept or call off the dog, at *all* costs, and with *all* expediency. Go, *go !* " Then he sighed and turned to the rest. " Adeline, you've a dodgy mind, re-configure the east Asian dividends and scrounge the ransom. Draft strategy, verbal only to me, in one hour; everyone else, except Communications, be gone to your appointed frolic and please appear frightfully seasonal to the outer world. Communications… "

Simon Chatsworth, the only remaining target, and the person thus-labeled, tried to look keen as he watched his mulled wine and midday rendezvous with the most shapely vixen ever to toil in the Royal Navy Museum, float out the door.

" …earn your bonus for pity's sake…spin something that looks like we here at B.A. are the very *fount* of Christmas cheer, choosing Ireland from our esteemed but less fortunate customers to benefit from humanitarian initiative, etc., etc., blah, ho-ho – *got me ?* "

The CFO managed to reach Prinsep almost immediately at *The Dockside*, a poor-man's peerage of wannabe Admirals, armchair militarists and self-ascribed movers and shakers. And Prinsep was indeed shaken, choking on his red wine before Sutcliffe half-finished. He'd been trying to reach Neale himself earlier, but his mobile was evidently dead or disconnected, and he had no idea where the lout was.

Prinsep's £100 shirt wilted and clung with sweat…

(20)

A brilliant day swept clear from the southwest...brought the hills within hand's reach – a day of unstable airs and high filmy clouds...glaze under the sun...beheld the blue of the Channel turn through polished silver and dulled steel to dingy pewter. A laden collier hugging the coast steered outward for deeper water, and across copper-coloured haze...saw sails rise one by one on the anchored fleet.

Kipling

Two days before Christmas, and cozied into an English cliff ! Marie lay on her back, hands locked comfortably behind her head, drifting and dreaming in a perfect wind-break scooped in the heather, bracken, and soft long grass. The world as she cared to see it, stretched outward from her toes.

Thoby still slept. From her perch on Afton Down, she was able to pick out their window back at the *Albion*, as Afton rose from the east tip of Freshwater Bay to balance – though hardly match – the grand upward roll of Tennyson Down from the opposite rim.

Turning her head to the right, Marie saw the cross they'd pranced under the previous night, and she smiled with the pride of a new owner. From there, her eyes tracked lazily down to the hotel, around the bay, out to the stacks of several 'Masefield' coasters on the horizon, and the glare-white sail of a single yachtsman. The ocean screen, played on by thin, hastening cloud and random funnels of light, oscillated in a hypnotic shimmer of hues.

After a while, like any child, Marie had to get up, carefully select ideal pieces of chalk, then hurl them out one by one, feeling giddy as she watched them waffle down 150 feet. Her missiles all fell short of where the slate skin of the ocean split, peeled into lime green and white foam by two rock pinnacles mimicking the 'Needles' at Alum Bay. The brief kaleidoscope, spent, slid away in deep Baltic blue far beneath Marie's feet. She stepped back, dizzy, and resumed her comfy post…

A tern shrieked so piercingly overhead that Marie jerked bolt upright in time to see the wing-shadow roll off her legs.

It had been a paradisial, almost erotic sleep. She had no idea how long she'd been there. Thoby might wonder, but he would find her. Everywhere there was 'their's' now – she'd laid respectful claim that very morning. You don't get lost at home…

The sea lurched and tilted when she got to her feet. She noticed for the first time a cairn or monument of some sort perhaps twenty meters from her roost, and curiosity led her to investigate before heading back. There was nothing of its kind anywhere else she'd seen on the cliffs, so Marie felt it wasn't likely a surveyor's mark; besides, it was national property.

It was a square stone, about four feet high and pointed at the top, inclined slightly towards the edge of the precipice a mere five to six feet away. At the instant she came up to it, the sun turned suddenly on the buttercups clustered at its base, momentarily dazzling her before she could decipher the facing inscription:

ELM
Aged 15

He cometh forth
Like a flower
And is cut down.
He fleeth alone as
A shadow and
Continueth not

Odd, thought Marie, a lone grave up there. She moved round the stone hoping for more of the story and found the sea-face inscribed:

ERECTED
IN REMEMBRANCE
OF A MOST DEAR
AND ONLY CHILD
WHO WAS SUDDENLY
REMOVED TO ETERNITY
BY A FALL FROM
THE ADJACENT CLIFF
ON THE ROCKS BENEATH

28 August 1846

*Not a grave then…*her immediate reaction, despite genetic queasiness at heights, was to peer over the fatal ledge, as if he might still be floating there. As she did so, her thighs turned to jelly and she had the sensation of being watched. The Down was devoid of humans as far as she could tell, but she leapt back so abruptly she tumbled to all-fours. *Could he have been pushed ?*

She imagined the fall, the scream and first thud, then rebounding, still conscious, doll-like into the wash below, and bobbing there till stranger, friend, or distraught family happened by…

Marie shuddered and clutched at some heather to ground herself. She looked down, seeking reassurance in signs of life, only to fasten on Thoby, plodding barefoot in her direction along the broad ribbon of beach, swerving whimsically in and out of the breakers' residue.

Marie stood tall and waved rhythmically with both arms, savouring life, *her* life.

**

Not a frigging peep from Neale; whereabouts a complete mystery.

Prinsep seethed. He bit his tongue and put out a wildly indiscreet APB to all Neale's watering holes, had his grotty digs in Belgravia ransacked, and feverishly tried his mobile every ten minutes, feeling the perfect idiot: 'The customer you have attempted to reach is currently not signed in…' Prinsep saw himself signed into the madhouse if he failed to spike his loose cannon.

'Just when the world's attention-deficit and extortion beg us to keep a low profile…' The Chairman's words rang in his ears, 'let's not hand it to them on a goddamned silver platter !'

Where was a 'leaves on the rail' disaster when you needed one? *If I can't stop him God, just tell me he's on a doomed train somewhere…*

Otherwise, the sole Plan 'B' was a faint hope Neale hadn't been able to pick up the couple's return trail.

**

Farringford,
December 23

" Welcome, welcome…best of the season…thanks for turning out – *glorious* weather ! " The Curator of the Cameron Trust stood in front of the blazing fire in the main foyer, jovially greeting one and all as they made their entrance onto the rich carpet.

Scarlet bows adorned the wood paneling, and coniferous boughs and sprigs of real holly from the estate were tucked along picture frames and up the banisters. A robust Scotch pine dripped with figurines, tiny white lights, and crimson and royal blue velvet bows.

Hynchcliffe was equally decked out in the spirit of the occasion, having plumped himself in leggings, high boots, an ornate silk vest and black frock coat, and a high wing collar wrapped with a green cravate.

There were 200 invited guests, principally the fresh cream and blueblood of British photography, who filed into the poet's manor, including two earls, an ex-royal romance turned queen of the shutter, a brace of Tennyson buffs and biographers, devotees of the 'Freshwater Circle', and twenty-five lucky members picked by lottery from the 'Friends of European Opera' society.

Evening dress prevailed, the majority of women wrapped in as little black as gravity permitted. Tables in the atrium off the dining room groaned with strawberries, chocolate ginger, champagne, and silver punch-bowls of egg-nog.

Sam Neale shuffled back and forth in the hallway in his all-purpose Armani. He wasn't a mixer in any sane sense of the word, but tonight he was doubly wired, the primary charge being to see and hear von Otter.

The general atmosphere bubbled, as did the Chairman of Parnassus Camera, underwriter of *Dimbola*'s current welfare and key sponsor of the event. He'd done his homework, and had chosen as introduction the Laureate's lines on an earlier state occasion.

" ...how wonderfully *à propos* that we greet the reigning mezzo soprano in our poet's home with the very words he wrote to welcome Princess Alix to England in 1863: '*Come to us, love us and make us your own*.' "

Neale squirmed at the gushy tone, entirely missing the allusion – so what if royalty had sung there before – but any thought was hijacked by the vision of Marie arriving in a barely-there, navy halter-top sheath. Her amber eyes sparkled, her face firm and glowing from hours traipsing the region.

It was the second sighting that day. Neale lacked a classical education, and thus proper knowledge of how the gods operate, but it was evident unseen forces were at work. He hadn't stopped twitching and grinning since the morning, and now that he watched Marie glad-handed by Hynchcliffe, the excitement generated by von Otter swelled with desire and vindication. His arid mien completely shed itself: the reptile undressed and poked into dancing by a hot desert bloom.

He almost questioned why he'd punted his professional and romantic agenda in the first place – all deference to the *diva bellissima*. But then, Neale felt entitled; he had it coming, and had obviously made the right choice. It wasn't blind faith, as he had none, but the sure assumption, he told himself, that the creature who could fan the ashes of…*whatever* it was that burned inside him, would naturally possess superior tastes. It was consequently no surprise at all she should reappear then and there. She'd really been 'invited' by the strength of his allure. Neale shuddered, and a giant strawberry squirted from his fingers into his champagne.

" Ooh ! I like it that way too… " confided a blousy maven who'd left the Geez at home.

Neale bleated something inaudible and slid off to a comforting pillar. From there he had a clear view over Marie's shoulders of von Otter, who was just introducing her accompanist. For a blindered, evil soul, the bonus in this gala and fortuitous scene seemed oddly difficult to digest: namely, *Carlyle*.

Here was his original target clasped by the woman's lovely arms, the means restored to shut down his faggy masters at British Andorra. Absolutely perfect. All he had to do was wait till they were separated, even momentarily. *Get him, take her…*

It was a given, but von Otter won the room outright with two sweeping Vivaldi arias back to back. She frolicked with the octaves, eye-balling helpless members of the audience while she lingered in awesomely low registers, and tickled everyone with her easy, seamless caricature. No tremor, no brassy tones, all crystal purity.

A Beethoven aria, *Hans Heiling*, followed; then as promised Bengt, *Six Songs* from Mahler's *Des knaben Wanderhorn*.

Neale stood pinned against the post, reduced to the village idiot, drooling between two goddesses, one his commanding voice, the other, the fleshly prodigal guarding his future.

Just before intermission, von Otter summoned two bronzed young Ecuadorans from the front row, armed with guitar and Panpipes. She turned her back, then stunned the audience by unleashing a protracted wail – heart-wrenching, but utterly beautiful – echoed, after what seemed an eternity, by the mournful breathiness of the pipes, then coaxed slowly into a more earthly, sensuous rhythm by the guitar. The lyric, sung in Spanish, haunted the room before trailing off in the jungles of lost love.

When the last note escaped and von Otter gazed over the chamber, she was *every* woman since time immemorial, leaving an emotional imprint so defined no one would have recognized the Viking deity.

" *Sans pareil* ", enthused Marie into a third glass. " Isn't she magnificent Thoby ! Can you believe we're here together for this ? The way it must have been so often… "

Thoby had to agree, and did so with a kiss behind her perfumed ear. Truly, he marveled at the undeserved, divine intervention in his life, even fantasizing how the two of them would someday preside over a new Freshwater Circle. But he couldn't dispel the present scene and the physical, closed-in feeling. He'd already scanned the gathering, wondering who might know or recognize him: his face had been all over the tabloids and media in recent months; every smile or nod threatened to put him back on the defensive. It gnawed quietly at the delicate icing on his Christmas cake.

Get a grip Carlyle, you're in heaven for Christ's sake, with an angel no less…

Thoby glanced longingly out the bank of east windows over a bucolic vista which rolled down through *Dimbola* and into the Bay. Deep purple thunderheads tumbled in off the ocean, colliding with the downs. A strong wind had apparently risen and the branches, in his view, beckoned. The chatter and festivity which at first had been exhilarating, receded with the string trio filling the interlude and Thoby felt even more constricted, edgy, as people began to file back to their seats. Life outside pulsated while he was trapped inside…He reminded himself he'd 'cleared' a possible exit with Marie. *A walk in the elements, on my own to face my own…solid idea.*

" ...just popping out to check the estate before the storm, " he whispered, " don't let it spoil our local debut… "

" Not to worry, *I'll* mind the guests, " Marie assured him, knowing he meant the Down.

" Be back soon though… " She leaned over wickedly, blinking her lashes, " and be careful dear heart, the village hounds are often loose up there. "

Marie watched Thoby dodge gratefully out the pantry door and bolt past the south-east corner. He had to be headed for the little foot-bridge Tennyson built over the common path in the woods to avoid passersby. She let the manicured jostle by as she stared after Thoby into the dark copse. Why did she feel apprehensive – she was profoundly content with things generally to say the least – perhaps, she admitted, hearing her grandmother's voice, *c'est que tu es folle d'amour, bien sûr.*

The involuntary sentiment tugged at Marie, reminding her how far she'd traveled since October. Gone were her advocate's chains, so ambitiously forged. In the same blast of chutzpah, she'd crossed an ocean and discovered people, alive *and* dead, who inspired curiosity and passion. She'd chanced on a kindred soul, running on impulse and shucking his curriculum vitae; one also missing a father, yet whose heroes waved a fresh, romantic banner. Her own origins, though not demeaned, had faded, now all but packaged and sent gently back as a once-upon-a-time way-station. And that man, despite rigorous criteria – *Jesus Murphy, Marie, he was a tobacco hack* – for whom she now cared, a *lot* – how in hell had *that* happened ! And so soon after taking vows of general disdain and self-indulgence…

Marie took a final gander out the window before heading back to her seat. She noticed a bland little man with thin hair and darkish complexion hunched forward, beetling off in the same direction as Thoby. Another fugitive from confined spaces…

" This next selection is a much-beloved aria by Giacomo Puccini, but I don't need to tell you wonderful people that ! It's inspired a bit of a challenge and I hope my attempt to meet it won't abuse your love of opera ! Joining me as the chorus are four talented students from your London Conservatory… "

Marie's head shot back and her body tightened into a single knot. That hunched form, that churlish attitude…her forensic knack kicked in to make the link: *the gallery at St. Paul's, the street corner in Chelsea after the break-in*. She leapt up, literally hurdling the stout woman's legs beside her and tore down the aisle and out the same exit as Thoby, sprinting for the Down.

Oh Thoby, how could we be so stupid ! There was absolutely no doubt, the one she dreamed of sharing this very ground with was in extreme peril. Pounding along in the growing horror of realization, Marie couldn't shake the absurd idom, '*It was a dark and stormy night…*'

A light mist turned to cold rain. The track was deeply rutted dirt and grass and Marie slipped constantly; she kicked her shoes off and ran on, neither man in sight.

And ah for a man to arise in me,
That the man I am may cease to be…
Forward, let the stormy moment fly
and mingle with the Past.
I that loathed, have come to love him.
Love will conquer at the last

Tennyson

The angry weather didn't faze Thoby; he wasn't turning back. Even prior to his ducking the affair, a *solo* visit to the cliff had urged itself eerily on his resolve. He shed the 'tellibly English' smoking jacket he'd worn to tease Marie, rolled it up, and tucked it under his arm. The navy turtleneck beneath seemed appropriately rugged. He hated the word 'closure'– everyone and their uncle seemed to crave it – but it was just a short hike, and Thoby was convinced that wisdom of some sort lay waiting…

When he came onto the Down, for the second time now, it struck him as raw and inhospitable compared with the day before, quite desolate without Marie. But the atmosphere was compelling; there was always the wild sea foaming away down below to make you feel safe on land, and when he stared up at the cross into the tumultuous sky, an immense calm gripped Thoby. He finally understood that any 'message' to be delivered up there must come from *him*.

With rivers of wine, voyage, and sensational loving, recriminations and desires had distilled substantially…*Dear father, you never knew me, which may have been a blessing, and I never knew you, which was my saddest loss. I tried so hard to outdo your heroics, and not hard enough to understand your sacrifice. In the end, I suppose I cheated and simply aimed at becoming such a blinding 'success' it would bury your wretched death. There's nothing to forgive you and everything I've done to your name to be accountable for – but I've made a start, however feeble. My shame can never be totally wiped clean; even you couldn't free your mate.* Thoby wasn't sure of the analogy but meant well. *Am I on an honourable course ? I mean, my efforts, this smashing woman – I think you'd love her too…*

Thoby lowered his gaze, over the ghostly 'Needles' in the near distance and out to the Solent, now masked completely in a film of icy turquoise. Only days ago, he'd sailed into this newer world. It was not too late…

The more Neale's pricey threads got damp and muddied, the purer and more focused he felt, and the more he grinned: the target was live, out there alone, and *not* coming back. As he wheezed along, he muttered out loud, 'they'll love *my* last song…I'll go out with a bang.'

It had never been the human misery per se, the cowering receipt when he delivered an executive ultimatum or an actual hit, which pumped Neale. Because his prior life was a plague that never retreated, shrouding every waking hour with its tattered failure, it was more the finality of action, the successful closing of a 'file' which gratified. Carlyle, however, posed something unique, and unquestionably, Neale relished his taking-down. First impressions in Surrey had only hardened after the whistleblower, babe in hand, had stolen back under Neale's proud radar.

He had no quarrel with the woman, just a besotted need for her company. That she'd stayed behind just then spoke volumes – maybe they'd had a fight, which made it even easier…

Neale bent over, gasping after the final grade onto the top, and peered cautiously from behind a shrub twenty meters from where Thoby stood. No one else was visible anywhere along the cliff. Indeed, caution might literally have been 'thrown to the wind' as the latter moaned and howled alternately, while the evening coastal light expired under the heavy ceiling.

Neale toyed with showing himself first, even thanking him for returning the woman. He scurried over to the left, crouching low, nearer the edge, where he would be squarely behind Carlyle.

Your wide eyes are the only light I know
from extinguished constellations

Tennyson

Rain swelled the tears of frustration. The bizarre twist in an idyllic journey lodged painfully in Marie's throat, and she cursed her naïveté. The grand tour had dulled a well-honed intuition – she blamed herself as his 'counsel' – whatever persuaded them they could escape detection ? Part of her beseeched the fates to yank them back to the concert and the soft tinkle of glass, but the only sound was her own grunting, her bare feet squishing into the cold path, and the wind gusting.

The same imagination which had suddenly divined the worst, worked overtime to feed her panic. Marie saw herself racing back in time, back to rescue Alfred and Julia: she'd draped herself in their legacy after all; it was her duty. To succeed, though, Thoby must survive.

All her native strengths surged together – mind, body, fierce fidelity – she felt like a living motto. In the anguish of the moment, it seemed not improbable she'd 'trained' all her life *expressly* to meet this melodrama. All it lacked in the growing tempest was a shivering pony, a stolid gamekeeper, and an evil, tormented soul – but her heart knew that soul already paced up ahead…

Marie scrambled up the final rise and barged onto the summit, terrified by what she might see, only to catch her breath as if clothes-lined, and instantly throw herself flat on the ground. Both men stood in front of her, in plain though rapidly dimming view. Thoby gripped the black iron fence at the base of the celtic marker, with his back to Marie, while the other man squatted at the cliff-edge behind and to Thoby's left. Two figures in an ominous painting.

The champagne had completely worn off. There was no calling '911'; this was *it*, however luck played it. An involuntary flash made Marie think of the Puccini aria climaxing down behind and centuries away: the prince's identity the fatal prize – but she'd no desire to learn who this man was; she already knew *what* he was.

In the next second, all bets were off. Like a nightmare, Marie watched the stalker slowly unbend and extract something from behind his waist. She strained to make out a handgun, one that was a ludicrous size for such a runt. He didn't point it right away, evidently pondering something, just as Thoby appeared totally rapt in some sort of communion at the cross.

Every instinct said to yell, but Marie jammed her teeth shut. There was no point. She was down-wind in a gale, and even if heard, would merely offer a second target. The sacrifice demanded by the moment was unequivocal, and drove her feet in two quick bursts, like a sodden cat ready to pounce, to within yards of Neale. How could he not notice ! But without some further 'damning evidence', it simply wasn't in Marie to push the final button, so she halted, totally exposed, waiting for the crisis.

A wraith of spume blew past her nose like smelling salts, then Neale raised the gun with both hands, having tired of the rain and Thoby's inattention. Marie catapaulted forward. Neale saw her at the last second, but was so shocked he didn't budge or change his aim.

" You ! " he garbled.

Marie's only weapon was the memory of a football heart-throb who insisted on teaching her how to throw a 'cross-block'. She dropped her head and launched herself, hip-first, at Neale, crashing into his knees and upending him. His chubby arms shot skywards, releasing his gun, but he struggled to get up immediately, ignoring both Thoby and the gun, his porridgy face strangely calm. The wind worked itself to a shrill pitch as Neale reached, almost robotically, into his right pants pocket.

There was an instant's hesitation as Marie judged the impasse she'd created, but she could only assume another gun, and hurled herself at Neale a second time. Her right shoulder slammed into him just below the breastbone. His whole body deflated, and actually bounced backwards. A piece of paper and a wisp of something sailed out of his hand into oblivion. His rear-end scraped the loose chalk, sliding only a few inches before he felt completely weightless.

He never looked away from Marie, and Marie could only stare back, frozen to the spot by what she had done, and by the slow, giant cartwheel of Neale's descent onto the broken shore. The final image, the now-remembered face, baffled his tortured eyes: that of his once-adoring wife, Andrée.

If there'd been any scream, the wind's roar hid it with a greater silence. Marie had uttered nothing herself, consumed by reflex. She was still on all-fours, hands propped in the depression just made by Neale's body. There was no need to look over, he was gone. She'd just killed another human.

The sight of the man twisting away lingered as Marie stood up – he *had* said something, a partial word only, a flat syllable. A nurse friend once told Marie how old men often cry out for their mothers at the moment of death. Neale had managed, 'Ma…', which didn't sound like 'mother' – though in French, '*Ma*man' fit, but there was nothing to suggest that here – and certainly not 'Marie'. They'd never met, not face to face.

Adding to the mystery was the bizarre emptying of his pocket even as he fell away…and then a hot shiver of guilt as it suddenly occurred he may not have been a corporate lackey after all. What if he'd just been a deranged parent of a young smoker burnt in a bedroom fire, fixating on Thoby from the media, an angel-father of revenge ? But that didn't fit; that gnarled individual had never been a parent, and, no matter who he was, he had clearly intended to murder Thoby.

Thoby !

Marie looked around, already making a conscious effort to keep the lid on her trauma, but the goof, as she peered towards the cross, had evidently missed the entire thing. The wind and dying light had helped obscure sound and motion, and the incident had occupied all of ten seconds. His life and death had been resolved without notice.

If she kept silent, would 'justice' be thwarted ? Did she honestly care ? Who frankly would ever know, or care to know – why would B.A. rush to claim its rat ? And for that matter, what point was there in telling Thoby – and Marie instantly determined, 'none'. This would be her gift, the muting of the past, a gesture which thereupon sealed the unmarked grave of Samuel Neale. The defense rested.

Marie calmly pushed the gun over the edge with her toes and began running, once more, towards her lover. As she 'fled the scene', she prayed the thing wouldn't go off against the rocks.

" Darling ! "

" You foolish… "

The vision of a hell-bent gamin in skimpy shift welded to her skin, tearing towards him in bare feet out of the mist, struck Thoby like a bolt of lightning from the storm he'd otherwise ignored.

" What ever… " he sputtered, but they hugged each other like the end-frame of a cheap movie and didn't speak for several minutes. Marie was drained and elated all at once, having vanquished the devil, while Thoby felt sheepish for having dragged his love into a wild night. “ I *did* promise to be back… ”

“ I know, but I suddenly worried and just took off – maybe I needed a run like you needed open space – *no*, the further I went, the more I got paranoid. I didn’t want to lose you to some…chance, or accident…I just *cared*, that’s all, and here I am, ” feeling freed by her admission.

“ Here we *both* are, we must be… ”

“ ‘Bonkers’ as you would say, ” and both erupted in hysterical laughter, acutely aware of the dramatic scene they posed.

On cue, the wind abated and the dark clouds streaked on to Sussex and Hamps. Marie began to tremble uncontrollably. Thoby massaged her feet, but she refused his loafers. He unfurled his jacket and wrapped her in it and they started back, taking the first opening off the backside, a steep, rather uneven path. They slipped frequently, but didn’t care, laughing and kissing.

“ I love you Robin. ”

“ I love you more Julia… ”

“ Sickening aren’t we ! ”

“ A wonderful thing to be… ”

Found and resurrected, Thoby raved to himself. Could life be better than sharing the scene behind them ? Their two silhouettes beneath the cross, against the backdrop of sea and swirling sky, hung themselves permanently over his heart's mantelpiece.

" I saw this place this morning when I was out walking early…just along from that shop at the fork. Classic thatched roof, *and* it has a name Thoby: 'Myrtle Cottage'! You'd love it and… "

" It's for sale – out in front of you for once Frenchie, not just another pretty face you know – and yes we'll buy it. The estate agent was charming on the phone… "

" You are disgustingly *sympa, toi* ! "

" Bang on dear heart, and won't it be the finest, most eclectic B&B anywhere, not to mention an inspiring headquarters for conspiracies to commit useful social unrest ! "

Farringford was now in sight and they held each other tighter, not minding their appearance in case anyone should look out. Marie smiled deep inside, vowing to write and invite her mom to come and visit amongst the spirits of so much goodness and greatness. Her father could rot in Switzerland, or wherever he existed...

The security guard at the front hall took a good minute to recognize and accept the bedraggled pair as invited guests. Marie looked the twenty-something lad in the eye, pointing at Thoby, and confided, " He gets quite overwrought at opera… "

Stifling giggles, Marie and Thoby headed straight for the champagne trays, where, as old novels put it, they '*set to with a will and quickly made short work'* thereof. The first of several decreasingly articulate toasts saluted Lord Alfred's photo, and its maker, over the fireplace.

No sign of the storm remained and a splendid moon sat kindly over the Bay. Drier and warmer, Marie and Thoby were drawn to the parlour windows, unable to stay away from the sight of their new homelands. Thoby was benignly regal in a plush leather armchair, with Marie standing behind him, bending over with her arms on his shoulders, lovingly tolerant. Maybe it was just losing the chill, but a glow suffused her whole body, as if Lilian warmed her with approval. As if Marie too, had brought one back…

Von Otter emerged briefly from the press of admirers and post-recital celebration. She looked quizzically at the couple huddled at the window for a second or two, not questioning their motley garb – they had come to hear her, which was wonderful in itself, and had apparently experienced something intense – then she turned away and murmured, " Beautiful… "

END

Postscript

British Andorra continues to print money.

The opera world, though wedded by nature to tragedy and twists of fate, has failed outright to mark Sam Neale's exit from the stage.

On auspicious weather days, which is almost always at Freshwater, Alfred and Julia still climb the downs, or pace along the sea-wall, conversing ardently between periods of passionate silence.

The keen observer will note their outward appearance does not resemble their well-known portraits.